James J. Owen

Gleanings in Various Fields of Thought

James J. Owen

Gleanings in Various Fields of Thought

ISBN/EAN: 9783741183751

Manufactured in Europe, USA, Canada, Australia, Japa

Cover: Foto ©Andreas Hilbeck / pixelio.de

Manufactured and distributed by brebook publishing software
(www.brebook.com)

James J. Owen

Gleanings in Various Fields of Thought

.

OUR

SUNDAY TALKS,

OR,

GLEANINGS IN VARIOUS FIELDS OF THOUGHT,

BY

J. J. OWEN,

Editor San Jose (Cal.,) Mercury

SAN JOSE:
MERCURY PRINTING AND PUBLISHING COMPANY
1883

PREFACE.

UNDER the general heading of "Our Sunday Talks," most of the matter of the following pages has appeared, from time to time, in the Sunday editions of the SAN JOSE DAILY MERCURY. The shorter articles and poems have also appeared in the same paper. Upon the solicitation of a number of readers, who seem to think these matters worthy of preservation in book form, I have here brought them together, revised and pruned of the crudities and imperfections that marred their first appearance,—written, as they usually were, like most of the editorials of a daily paper, under the spur, with but little time for reflection, and none for revision. In this second edition I have added a large number of new topics, thereby giving the work a more comprehensive scope. Hoping that these "Talks" may be received in the friendly spirit in which they were uttered: and further, that they may be the means of helping some struggling soul to clearer views of life and duty, this little volume is sent forth to the world by

THE AUTHOR.

INDEX.

OUR SUNDAY TALKS.

INTRODUCTORY.

WE wish it understood that these "talks" are from a secular standpoint wholly, and are intended to be entirely free from dogmatism or assumption of any kind. We shall aim to impinge on no one's private belief —offend no one's conscience. There is a common ground upon which all right thinking people can meet and agree; there are a thousand topics and themes affecting the welfare of humanity, concerning which no creeds can divide honest minds. It is in this vast field of thought we shall meet you, reader, as a friend and a neighbor, hoping you may find something in our "talks" to interest, if not instruct.

We have analyzed closely the motives that govern human action—have thought much of the frailties and weaknesses of human nature, and sought to fathom their causes—have sought to determine why it is that one man preys upon, and another seeks the welfare of, society. Whatever conclusions—partial only at best—we may have reached, our researches into this mystic realm of causation—of moral forces—have taught us a lesson of charity for human imperfections, a larger exercise of which in the world would, we believe, start the race a long way in the direction of that "good time coming," which has been the dream of the prophet and the inspiration of the poet, in all ages of the world.

Goodness we find to be all one thing, whether practiced by saint or sinner, pagan or Christian ; except that it is, perhaps, a higher virtue when practiced by one who counts on no reward therefor. And evil is the same in quality the world over, no matter what the belief or profession of the individual may be who practices it. The measure of merit or demerit in the exercise of either, depends upon many circumstances. We have

no right to expect apples of thorns nor figs
of thistles. Neither should we expect too
much of human thorns and thistles. We see
that wrong abounds on every side, and it is as
inscrutable to us as it is that death should lay
its icy hand upon the young, or that the pestilence should walk in darkness ; or that the
earthquake, the tornado, or the fierce lightnings, should desolate the homes of men.

We believe that all reformatory effort, to
insure success, must contain the elements of
a broad sympathy and a tender compassion
for those whom it is intended to benefit.
This is the secret of success in parental government, and it lies at the basis of all sub-
stantial elevation of the people of a state or
nation.

We know it is claimed that parents are
responsible for the quality of character of
their children. To some extent this is no
doubt true, but that they are not wholly so
is as true as that they are not entirely
responsible for their own characters. The
best of parents, often, have the most unruly
children ; while children who are left to come
up as best they may, often make grand and

noble men and women. We are satisfied
that the most effective of all parental discipline is the loving word spoken from a heart
full of sympathy. If that will not keep the
feet of the erring child from straying, nothing
else will.

Hence we conclude that in the exercise of
charity and brotherly love lies the hope and
salvation of the race.

BEGINNING TO WALK.

MEN ought to grow wiser as they grow
older. Some do. Others do not. All
who have profited by the garnered experiences of time—who have mingled much with,
and learned the ways of, the world, the
flesh and the devil, and of the church also;
and who, above all, are actuated by that
spirit of kindness and charity that should prevail in our dealings with our fellow beings,—
all of this class will agree with us that a blind
and unreasoning opposition to the estab-

lished religious methods for the world's redemption is not wise.

One may believe all systems of religion to be false—as the outgrowth of barbarism, or as founded in the ignorance and superstition of man's undeveloped nature,—and yet he can not intelligently deny that there is a necessity for religious restraint over the minds and actions of men—of some men, of many men —not all, perhaps ; but of such a large percentage of the race as to make the maintenance of the church, in its varied forms of worship, an essential if not the main prop of society.

It may be, as is held by most so-called free thinkers, that if all religious teaching was supplemented by proper instruction in the laws of health, sobriety and right living— that if science was made to take the place of faith and revelation—better general results would follow than are now witnessed. This is extremely doubtful, for the reason that the average man lacks the capacity for philosophical application of the truths of science. The lessons of nature and the laws of life are nothing to him. He can only be reached, and that often indifferently, through his fears ; or stimulated to right action through his hope of reward. It is with this somewhat seriously damaged article of humanity—the average lot, which most people will concede is a bad lot—that society has to deal, for it is the lower stratum of this disagreeable average that causes society the most trouble.

He who derides all church influences and religious teachings would hardly care to reside in a community where there were no such influences and teachings—unless he was permitted to select his neighbors, which would scarcely be possible. Churches and grog shops may exist side by side ; and yet most persons who take no stock in either, would rather the two should exist together, than that the grog shops should have it all to themselves. It is only the inconsiderate and unreasoning infidel—the one with but one idea, and that badly demoralized—who would pull down the churches and destroy at a blow the pious faith of their devout membership.

The human race is yet in its infancy—is only beginning to walk. It needs all the helps and encouragements of religion as well

as science to keep it from stumbling ; and
they are not always sufficient. Although
groping amid shadows it is ever reaching out
after and struggling for the light. And it
will find it sometime—the true light—the
electric light of Wisdom. The law of eternal
progress is graven in the heart of the rock,
of the plant, of man. All life is barbed with
a divine purpose, ever penetrating and reaching forward, holding fast to that which it
gains, and never going backwards,—that is, in
its entirety and ultimate.

And so we welcome all helps to growth,
spiritual or intellectual—we care not whence
they come—whether from saint or sinner,
Jew or Gentile, Pagan or Christian. He is
our brother who loves his fellow men, and
would do unto them as he would that they
should do unto him—who strives by word
and act to so live that when death shall have
placed its icy seal upon his lips, the fragrance
of many a tender memory will penetrate the
hearts of those who knew him best.

TRULY honest minds do not differ as widely
as they are apt to think they do.

LEARN TO WAIT,

IFE has many puzzling problems—many
that stagger reason, and leave the mind
lost in a labyrinth of doubt. We can not
tell why it is that wrong is permitted to exist
in the world—that the innocent should suffer
for the wickedness of others—that nature, in
her operations, should seemingly be so inharmonious and make so many blunders,—
especially while we have, as we are taught
to believe, an all-wise and infinitely just Ruler
at the helm of the Universe. We can not
understand these things. No one can. The
least we can do is to wait patiently until we
can obtain clearer views of life. Sometime
and somewhere, we doubt not, we shall be
able to take in at a glance the whole long
journey of life, from the cradle to the grave.
Then we shall see, perhaps, in that clearer
light; that what seemed to us wrong here was
so only in seeming ; and that at last, and in
the eternal purposes of the Infinite, all is for
the best. We can not judge of the year by a

single day, nor of a human life by a single experience. We must see the first in its completeness, and live the other through all of its experiences, to judge correctly of either. Then when we feel it in our hearts to complain or rebel at our lot—at the hard conditions to which we are sometimes subject— would it not be well to wait a little while before we sum up the case and conclude that Nature is out of joint?

" KNOW THYSELF."

"KNOW thyself" is one of the oldest maxims of the race. It is a piece of advice, however, that but very few people comparatively ever profit by.

Most persons have only a sort of speaking acquaintance with themselves—as though they lived next door neighbor, or across the street. They never come into full and loving sympathy with their own natures, and hence never realize of what treasures of sweet and beautiful companionship they deprive themselves.

To know one's self thoroughly requires much more patient research and study than most people would imagine. But no knowledge is fraught with such rich rewards to its possessor—such perfect argosies of wisdom and happiness.

First come the delights of that physical knowledge which makes us familiar with the hidden springs and secrets of life—with the quality and functions of every nerve, organ and muscle—with all the wonderful mechanism and movements of the " house we live in." But this knowledge is only a stepping-stone to those higher joys that come of intimate relationship with, and keen insight into, the character of that mysterious occupant of this earthly temple, the living soul.

Here is indeed a vast field for research— a mighty storehouse of treasure—or trash, and sometimes both. To add to the former, and to cast out and displace as much of the useless and worthless as possible, should be every one's life work.

The chief aim of life with many people

seems to be to devise ways and means for getting away from themselves. They are miserable when alone, and are only reasonably contented when entertained and amused by someone else. Such people may be very kind hearted and very good, in their way, but they are often terrible vampires to their friends—absorbing their lives and giving nothing in return.

A well stored brain never tires of its own company. It finds food for thought in a thousand things whereof the superficial mind would take no note. The worn pebble by the roadside leads it back æons agone to the time when the foundations of the hills were laid. The down on a butterfly's wing opens up to it a wonderland of beauty and admiration. It looks out into the starry spaces, and down into its own infinite capacity for growth and enjoyment, and it can find no time nor place in all God's universe for loneliness.

We pity the man or woman who has never made the acquaintance of him or herself— who find no solid enjoyment in the fellowship and communion of their own souls. They are travelers who have missed their way—miners who never delve beneath the outcroppings of things, and know nought of the priceless wealth stored away in the solid vein below.

In the great battle of life he succeeds best who relies most upon himself. But one must be on most intimate terms with himself —must know well the scope of his powers —the strength and length of his good right arm,—or the blow he aims at the foe may fall short of the mark, or at best prove impotent for good.

Not but that association has its grand uses in the development of character—in fact is absolutely necessary to the proper culture and unfoldment of the mind,—the point we would make is that solitude and meditation are also important factors in the growth of the soul ; and that one's own best friend and companion,—the one of whose society he should be the last to tire,—should be—HIM-SELF.

* HE gets the greatest satisfaction, often, out of life, who does the largest amount of attending to his own business.

IT is a good thing for the world that we do not all think or act alike ; and that all do not possess the same amount of intelligence, wealth, or ability to wrestle with the problems of life.

We are too apt to look upon this life as the end of existence, rather than as the means to higher uses and ends to be employed and enjoyed in the hereafter. As an end we would naturally look for and desire completeness ; whereas, as a schooling and experience necessary to proper soul growth—as all-essential to the building up and rounding out of character—as a training school preparatory for the life and work BEYOND—we apprehend it is just about as it should be.

If all were good, there would be no opportunity for missionary work—no need of Churches, nor Sunday Schools, nor Young Men's Christian Associations. If all were rich, well-fed and contented, there would be no opportunity for the exercise of charity—no one to do the work of the world—nothing to stimulate effort and enterprise.   If there were no sickness, suffering nor sorrow in the world, there would be nothing to call forth the tender sympathies of humanity.   In fact, if there were no storms nor tempests of the soul we should never know how to appreciate the restful calm and sunshine—the joy that comes of gentle peace.

Hence, while the philanthropist, Christian and philosopher, are constantly studying methods for the amelioration of the condition of the race, and the advancement of humanity, 'the necessity for such work is as essential to the doer as it is to those who are done by. Sin and salvation, sickness and health, plenty and poverty, storm and sunshine, crime, cruelty, insanity and wrong ; life, growth, death and decay,—are all important factors in the development of character and the true growth of the soul.   He who fails to profit by these lessons, wastes the golden opportunity of his days.   He is a laggard and a truant in the primary school of life —an encumberer of the ground—profitless seed cast by the way-side.

This view of life is necessary to reconcile us to an endurance of life's ills. It teaches us to take things as we find them and make the best of them—to stop quarreling with our surroundings, and mourning over what can not be helped; but rather to set ourselves diligently at work to improving the conditions and circumstances in which we are involved. If there are brambles and rocks in our pathway, instead of sitting down placidly and deploring the fact, we should realize the necessity for greater personal efforts in making the way smoother for those who may follow; and with ready heart and hand we should lend ourselves to the work.

So will life become sweeter from duty performed, and we shall mount heavenward as we grow into the image of a better manhood.

THE man who demands a single civil, social, or political privilege for himself that he would not accord to his wife, mother, sister or daughter, possesses the rudimentary principles of a tyrant, although he may not think so.

HUMAN SYMPATHY,

IN the struggle and battle of life there is no one strong enough to brave the contest alone. All need sympathy and help, and they must have it, or sure disaster and defeat will overtake them.

He who thinks himself strongest, when his life bark rides gaily before the breeze, with sails filled with the winds of prosperity, is often the weakest of the weak when the storm and the tempest come. Thus in the hour of sorest trial many a weak woman has often been strong and brave to endure, where stalwart manhood has succumbed and drifted helpless and discouraged before the the gale of adversity.

Life is sweetened and made beautiful by sympathy. Its asperities are toned down and its rough places made smooth by the touch of a gentle hand and the tone of a loving voice. Even its severest trials may be endured and its heaviest burdens borne, when aided by a very little thoughtful and precious help of this kind.

Suffering seems to be the common lot of all keen natures. The finer and more delicately strung the instrument the greater the liability to get out of tune, and when out of tune the harsher the discords.

Some people 'are so evenly organized in their natures that scarcely any amount of trouble worries them. Their lives flow on smoothly and serenely, but never deeply. As they are incapable of great sorrow, so also are they dull to the rapture of great joy. Emotionless souls—calmly placid natures,— in the wonderful unfoldments of human life, though they may be the wiser and happier, yet they can never be great natures. They approximate too nearly the dull and insensate conditions of life that belong to the earlier and lower developments of the race.

It is only the most intense natures that live most—that get out of life its grandest, if not best results—its highest happiness, although not unmixed, often, with its keenest agonies. In order to fully and truly appreciate heaven it is necessary to know what hell is made of.

All genius, whether in art or letters, belongs

to this intense class. In the sanctum, forum, pulpit,—in poetry, painting, sculpture, song, —in all the higher ways of mentality,— though often erratic, and sometimes weak in certain elements of character, they neverthe- less constitute the lightning strikers of the world. They are the men and women who mould public tastes, and shape the plastic thought of humanity into beautiful shapes. They often lead where they do not walk, and point out shining ways for other feet than their own to tread ; but they are none the less great in those attributes of soul and character that make them the heroes, instruct- ors and saviors of the race.

Such natures are but little understood by the great multitude, and they never can be fully understood in this life. Perhaps they will be better known and appreciated in the Beyond, when the masks and rubbish of earth shall be left behind, and the pure gem of soul shall find a better setting.

Why it is that from souls capable of these great conflicts—of struggles in fathomless depths of sorrow and transports on mountain heights of gladness—are mainly evolved the

highest fruitions of heart and brain, is something we can not understand. We must
wait till the veil shall be rent asunder, and
then we shall see and know—perhaps.

MODEST DOUBTERS,

TO the materialist the physical world is
the all in all of the universe. He sees
reality only in those coarser forms of matter
that appeal to the physical senses. In fact
he denies the existence of any and everything that his senses can not grasp, forgetting
that there may be keener senses than those
of his own organism. We use the term
"coarser forms of matter," because to the
undeveloped mind, those are the only forms
that impinge upon the senses. But science
is constantly unfolding new and imponderable
forms of which the senses take no note.
Traversing the field of matter it enters a new
and unexplored domain which seemingly lies
outside the boundaries of matter. And here

in a maze of subtile forces and forms, the unfolded mind is lost in wonder and reverence.

It is not our purpose to attempt to clear up the mists that hover over the border land of the physical. We desire merely to suggest that we can know but very little of the matter at best. In the aggregation of atoms of which our densest solids are formed there is in reality no permanence or solidity. In the crucible—under the action of other elements —these solids disappear in impalpable vapor, or enter into new forms. By an expansion of its internal heat, or that of the central orb around which it revolves, the ponderable globe itself might be resolved into the vaporous nebula whence it sprung. So, may it not be that what we call matter is the mere expression of force ; or rather force taking upon itself tangible shape ? That the things which seem to us the most tangible and real are in fact the most evanescent and unreal ; while the unchanging and everlasting belong exclusively to the domain of the imponderable ; or as we prefer the term, the spiritual ?

Therefore we should be modest in our

denial or rejection of what we do not know to
be true. There is very little, comparatively,
that we can know of anything save the
simplest rudiments. Whoever dogmatically
asserts that a thing is not so, because he
does not know it to be so, simply advertises
his ignorance to the world. And nowhere
among men is this dogmatism more pronounced than among a certain class of ministers of the Gospel, who, while they claim to
believe in the intelligent existence of the
spirit of man after death, nevertheless deny
all of the alleged phenomena relating thereto
—phenomena to the reality of which many of
the most eminent scientists the world has
ever produced have borne and do now bear
witness.

The best and clearest thinkers are never
dogmatic. They assert only after the most
thorough investigation and irrefragible proof ;
and they always deny cautiously. They
take nothing for granted that does not have
the approval of reason. Whoever abandons
reason casts overboard his compass and chart.
True, the former may be deflected by natural
bias, by false education, by various causes ;

and the latter may fail to indicate many a sunken reef and dangerous whirlpool, yet they are the best and really only guides we have—unless we choose to surrender all individuality and become puppets and pliant putty in the hands of other minds. It is better to walk and stumble than not to walk at all.

The mind once awakened to the consciousness of the fact that this life is not the all of existence ; that it is merely a primary school to a higher grade beyond ; this conclusion reached, not as a matter of faith, which is often unreasoning and blind, but of absolute knowledge, and life has a new meaning, beauty and grandeur, of which the cold materialist never dreamed. The soul, hungry for spiritual food, demands of the ministers of religion of every faith this knowledge, the absolute proof of the soul's immortality. It will not be put aside with an evasive answer. It says, Give us the proof or stop preaching the doctrine ;—or at least stop denying the claim of those who think they know that "if a man die he shall live again."

BUT few people comparatively are "born to the purple." And it is a serious question whether those who are thus born, and are thereby relieved from a large measure of the cares and anxieties common to the world's toilers, are any better off therefor. The faculties of our natures that are not brought into constant and active play become limp and ineffective from disuse. Thus the man born to an inheritance of plenty misses all of those grand lessons of self-denial, and necessity for patient and persistent industry, that can be learned only in the schools of Adversity and Poverty. He misses the schooling of those hard struggles with the perplexing problems of existence, so necessary to harden his muscles, moral as well as physical, and bring out the best that is within him.

It is natural for the poor to envy the lot of the rich—especially of those who live in luxurious ease, and who, in the words of

Scripture, "toil not, neither do they spin,"—
the world's inutilities—the pampered descendants of sires who, in all their busy lives,
knew no rest nor peace of mind in the mad
acquisition of wealth, which did them but
little if any good, and their descendants
positive evil. If the poor only knew it, they
are better off as they are ; that is, so long as
they are prompted to struggle for something
beyond their present lot, and are reasonably
happy even though they fail to reach it.
The struggle for it, is the main thing needed
—it keeps the metal bright, and the faculties
in tune. No one can afford to go through
life without experiencing the necessity for
calling into constant and vigorous action all
his mental powers. Where the necessity is
wanting the faculty will be apt to lie dormant.

The hardest worked men in any community are those who devote their lives solely
to the acquisition of wealth. By constant
practice and application they succeed in
developing the acquisitive faculty to an
abnormal extent, at the price often of all the
nobler attributes of the soul. Such lives are
usually empty of sunshine. They are beyond

the pale of human sympathy,—are desolate
and unloved in the midst of plenty. True
growth is even growth—growth in all noble
directions. Large acquisitiveness should be
accompanied with large charity, large manliness of character. And yet the development of these traits of character seldom go
hand in hand. The race of Howards and
Peabodys is not so numerous as to be overcrowded.

Probably the worst condition of mind in
which a man can find himself is that of being
contented and satisfied with but little or
nothing. This is the other extreme of life.
It is to be practically worthless to himself and
to the world. Only those succeed in doing
who try to do. Infinitely better to try and
fail than not to try at all. To float with the
stream is the easiest thing in the world ;—to
stem and overcome it, and rise superior to it,
ah, that takes nerve and manhood. And
here is where nature draws the line between
the good and the good-for-nothing.

We should aim to be satisfied only with
what we can not help or improve. And
there is but very little with which we come in

contact, in our surroundings and circumstances, that we can not improve, if we have the will to set ourselves about it. If we lack the will, the sooner we cease to encumber the earth, the better for the earth.

KEEP OUT OF THE RUTS,

IF you would make rapid progress in the direction of truth keep out of the ruts.

We need to revise our opinions occasionally—politically, socially, religiously, and otherwise,—just as we need, from time to time, to reset our watches, or adjust the variation of our magnetic needles.

We form our conclusions upon any given subject from the evidence before us at the time. We may not always be in possession of all the facts in the case. We may find that we have placed too much stress upon *this* point and not given *that* sufficient importance. Hence, we are liable to err, even the wisest of us ; and we notice that those generally err the most who think they err the least.

It is this natural and inevitable tendency to imperfection and incompleteness of judgment that prompts the truly wise man to be extremely cautious in his assertions of fact— that induces him to hold the case open till the testimony is all in. And in whatever relates to the unknowable, or purely speculative, it is never all in, and no finality can be reached in this life.

The man who never changes his opinions is apt to be more stubborn than wise. In time he gravitates into a sort of mental groove or rut and becomes bigoted and dogmatic. He is in the position of a judge who closes the case on trial before him before the evidence is all in, and jumps at a conclusion that may not be warranted by the ultimate facts.

Of course, there are demonstrable facts concerning which the case may be considered closed—such as the facts of nature and of science that have long since ceased to be regarded as theories. Our conclusions on these points may be regarded as completed —as needing no further revision,—and they may be properly labeled and packed away in the storehouse of the brain. It is not about these facts that men are apt to differ greatly, for the means are always at hand to prove the correctness of their opinions. It is the long array of unprovable things concerning which they wrangle, and pull hair, and call each other hard names.

The time was when to doubt was to be socially and eternally damned—when to be a skeptic was to subject oneself to the pains of the rack and thumbscrew. In the better light of an advancing civilization that mode of enforcing belief was supplemented by milder, but no less objectionable methods—social ostracism—which, to a sensitive mind, is often less endurable than physical torture.

It takes a brave heart and resolute will to stem the popular current, when the multitude say, "Crucify him." But in all ages such there have been, and to them we are indebted for the liberty of opinion we enjoy to-day.

Honest skepticism no longer subjects one to the rack, in any sense. The conscientious doubter can walk erect among, and command the respect of his fellows—even of those who think, or think they think, that he will have a

place among the eternally lost in the life to
come.

Our best enlightened religious teachers
are no longer offensively dogmatic in the
presence of intelligent unbelief. And the
latter is inclined to be modestly unobtrusive,
except when aroused. We are learning to be
more respectful towards each other—more
considerate of each other's tender spots.
And this is as it should be. It enables us to
get along much more harmoniously than we
otherwise could. It is a sort of moral lubri-
cating oil, making less friction in the attrition
of ideas.

And all this comes of the liberalizing
influence of modern things, and of our
improved modes of thought. We are living
in an age and times when thoughtful men
have something else to think of than the
speculative problem of existence beyond the
boundaries of time. They realize the importance of a better order of NOW, and find too
much to do in the ever pressing needs of the
present, and in the common battle of life, to
waste too much force and substance on what
may interest us more, perhaps, by-and-by.

SOMEWHERE.

TIRED hearts that go life's rugged ways alone,
    Somewhere, in God's vast universe of soul,
    In realms of light, where law and love control,
Each one shall find its own,
        Somewhere.

O, think not this the all of life, below.—
    Its cares and burdens, agonies and tears,
    That weigh the soul through many weary years,
Full recompense shall know,
        Somewhere.

Nature with all her children fairly deals.
    All time is hers, and boundless realms of space,
    And endless means, and ways we may not trace,
Her purpose she reveals
        Somewhere.

We may not see the justice of her ways,
    Nor know why wrong prevails, or sin endures,
    Nor why to evil deeds the tempter lures.
The very doubts we raise,
        Somewhere

Will turn to golden fruit ; our pray'rs and tears
    Shall blossom into joys, whose fragrance sweet
    Shall make the fullness of our lives complete,
And banish all our fears,
        Somewhere.

If this were all, and death the final goal,
  And all outreaching aspiration dies,
  When 'neath the clod the mortal casket lies,
And dwelleth not the soul
    Somewhere—

Then were Nature's purposes in man
  Exceptional to all her perfect ends :
  Our very being's incompleteness lends
Failure to her plan,
    Somewhere.

FREEMASONRY OF BRAINS.

IT is related of those sweet, white-souled sisters, Alice and Phœbe Cary, that their pretty, modest home was the frequent resort of many of the literati of New York City. Horace Greeley, Park Benjamin, Bayard Taylor, and other famous men of letters, often met at their cosy little tea parties; and we can well imagine the "flow of soul," the brilliant conversations, the sparkling wit, the interchange of noble thought, and the flashing emanations of genius, that must have made those meetings occasions of rare delight to each and all.

Thus we find among cultured people gen
erally, in their social relations, a larger freedom from conventional restraint, and a more
profound contempt for the opinions of "Mrs.
Grundy," than among those of shallower
intellectual depths. They constitute a sort
of Freemasonry of brains, a Guild of Soul,
the shibboleth to which can only be spoken
with proper accent by those born to the
purple. Conscious of the rectitude of their
lives and the genuineness of their characters,
they do not trouble themselves much about
their reputations, for that they know often
consists only of the breath of fools. Faithful
to the divinity within their own souls, they
recognize the pure gold of character and the
right royal stamp of intellectual and spiritual
worth wherever they find them; and, if at
all, they naturally seek for the friendship and
companionship of their kind. Thus they are
apt to be misunderstood by the thoughtless
and superficial, especially when these pure
intellectual friendships exist between those of
opposite sexes outside the marital relations.
As though intelligent people could not with
propriety enjoy such friendships, and the

refining attrition of mind with mind which
follow therefrom, without subjecting themselves to the censure of that prurient prude
that sometimes goes by the name of Society.
When will the world learn that the mind is
sexless—that genius is a thing of the
immortal spirit—that in the higher life of
the soul there is "no marriage nor giving in
marriage."

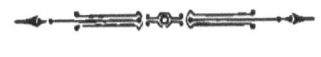

CONTENTMENT,

ONE of the chief studies of mankind in all
ages has been how to obtain the most
for the least,—in other words, how to get
the most money for the least labor ; and the
largest measure of happiness for the smallest
amount of effort.   This is a right principle ;
provided, that in getting the most we do not
trespass on the rights of the least ; and provided further, we make the right use of what
we get.   Upon these two points hinge all the
equities and virtues of the accumulation of
wealth.

One source of almost unlimited trouble in
this world is in not knowing when we are
well off. Our happiness depends too much
on what we suppose others may think of us,
and too little on what we really think of
ourselves. We carry the spirit of rivalry
and emulation to an extreme. In our efforts
to excel our neighbors we often overdo the
business and make ourselves miserable.

Where is the early pioneer of any new
country who will not tell you in his old age
that life was sweeter to him, and his happiness more complete, away back in his log
cabin days, when his neighbors, like himself,
were all poor and struggling with the wilderness for the bare necessaries of life, than in
his later years, in his palatial home, with his
body Brussels, French cooks, bay windows,
servants, rheumatism, pianos, and fashionable
grown up daughters. Not but that a beautiful home with pleasant surroundings is of
itself a source of pleasure to any refined
nature ; but to be conducive of true happiness
to the possessor it must be the natural outgrowth of culture and refinement, rather than
the creation of blind wealth to gratify a mean

spirit of rivalry or selfish vanity. It is the insatiate longing to excel—not in the gentle virtues of humanity, nor in the rich treasures of knowledge, but in mere temporal things that perish in a day—that plays the mischief with modern society.

There was a time in the not distant past when fortunes, except in rare instances, were acquired only by a lifetime of arduous and persistent struggle in some of the great industries of the world. Now, by the rise and fall of stocks fortunes come and go with the tide, leaving wrecks of humanity thickly strewn along the shores of time—for men are as often wrecked with riches as with their loss. Hence, it is no particular virtue, or even evidence of peculiar acquisitive skill, in these days, to acquire wealth. Many of our rich men are monuments of meanness and moral obloquy. They live by driving hard bargains, by grinding two per cent a month out of poor men, and foreclosing mortgages on the homesteads of widows. There is no more milk of human kindness in their natures than there is fragrance in a toadstool. The joy of helping others is a sensation they never knew. Their hearts are a nest of spiders eternally on the search for flies. They pile up riches, and their avarice grows upon what it feeds, until each avenue of their souls becomes the hungry mouth of a cuttle fish, sucking and absorbing from everything with which it comes in contact. When such men die it is a good thing for the world —perhaps. What such souls can find to do in the Land of Souls,—if there be any such place,—is something that no man can find out.

How much better for all if all were better content with their lot, and learned to cease envying the fancied happiness and enjoyment of others. The flowers that blossom in our neighbor's garden—their fragrance and beauty are as much for us as for their owner. We have a fee simple in just as much sunshine and air as he. We own just as large a patch of God's blue sky—can number among our jewels just as many stars as our more wealthy neighbor. Yes, infinitely more than he, for we are less encumbered with those worldly cares that obscure the glorious vision of the soul, and shut out the heaven that unfolds its broad expanse all around the humblest of earth's children.

————◦◦◦❈◦◦◦————

UNSOLVED PROBLEMS.

————

SOCIETY has to deal with many unpleasant facts—facts of pauperism, hoodlumism, intemperance, insanity, theft, murder, unfaithfulness in office, marital inharmony, and unbounded rascality of all kinds. These are facts which no amount of preaching, or legislation, or civil restraint, seems potent enough to avert, or even to modify. They exist everywhere to curse the better portions of the race, and fill the world with inharmony and tears. What to do with all of this diseased and disordered humanity—how to lick it into healthy and pleasant shapes—has been the puzzle of the ages. It is a problem that may well stagger the social scientist and philosopher of all times and climes.

This disagreeable fact is one that there is no sort of use in scolding about ; we must meet it, with all its unpleasant consequences, and we may as well be good natured about it as otherwise. It piles up huge burdens of taxes against the industrious and thrifty classes, which they may as well pay cheerfully as grudgingly; for fretting will not mend the matter, but rather sour the disposition and impair the digestion. We can't kill off these excrescences; law and humanity would not permit of it; and so we do what we consider the next best thing; that is, we maintain an expensive judicial system, and build vast court houses, asylums and prisons for their punishment and confinement, and for our own protection. But this works no cure of the evil. It simply lops off some of the branches without removing the roots, and two new shoots spring forth where one existed before.

We unhesitatingly assert, and challenge successful contradiction, that modern society, with its innovations in the matter of labor saving machinery, with its speculating tendencies, with its legislation favoring the accumulation of vast wealth in the hands of the greedy and strongly acquisitive few, is pauperizing and criminalizing the race at a rate unprecedented in the history of the world. Under this condition of things only the few can succeed, and the many, or a large and less acquisitively constituted portion thereof, must necessarily starve, steal or die. To tell the poor man, without a dollar in the world, and perhaps without the faculty for acquiring a dollar beyond his daily or immediate needs, that there are unoccupied government lands in Texas, Arizona or Montana, inviting him to emigrate thither, is of about as much use as to assure him that there are good farming lands in the planet Saturn that he can have for the asking. What the average poor man wants is work for wages. Deprived of this he becomes an outcast, a tramp, and perhaps a criminal. It is the duty of society to furnish him with employment—not employment for to-day and none for to-morrow ; but steady labor, at such remunerative wages as shall provide him with wholesome food, comfortable clothing and proper shelter, But how can society do this with muscle everywhere supplemented by machinery? The question is much more easily asked than answered.

We have reached an era in our civilization that is new and startling—one that the political or social economist of even a quarter of a century ago never dreamed of. He never dreamed that the time would come in the history of our nation and race when brawn and sinew would be the drug in the market that they are to-day. He never imagined that any element could so derange the adjustment of labor to bread, as that we witness to-day as the outcome of the uses of machinery in the industrial affairs of the world. The question to him is as new as it is momentous. It is one full of danger to society and the commonwealth.

With these facts before us what is the duty of the hour? In the first place the condition of the unemployed classes calls for the exercise of a broad spirit of charity and humanity on the part of the affluent. It should suggest to the latter that there is danger in the parsimony that permits of large numbers of idle men in the community. They should not only, in a private capacity, endeavor to furnish employment to the unemployed, but they should consent to the inauguration of public enterprises requiring many laborers.

And yet all these are but make-shifts—temporary expedients—flags of truce, as it were, to enable society to gather wisdom and strength to grapple with its greatest enemy, over-population.

How few people are well understood, even by their most intimate friends. We think we know them, but there is a sense in which those we know best are strangers to us. There are chambers in every human soul into which not even the eyes of our best beloved are ever permitted to gaze—thoughts and emotions that none are ever allowed to share. We see where the tide breaks in crested billows upon the strand; we hear the fierce roar of the tempest; we note the angry glare of the red lightning as it leaps from cloud to cloud; but the vast unfathomed universe of soul lies beyond, an impenetrable profound, unapproached and unapproachable forever.

USES OF TEMPTATION.

WE sometimes think, in the efforts of our temperance friends to reform the world from the evils of intemperance, and in which they usually lay all the blame upon the liquor-seller, that they do not fully appreciate the importance of temptation, as one of nature's means of testing the true metal and value of men. The occasional and moderate drinker—the inebriate and downright sot,—are all apt to be regarded as the innocent and helpless victims of the rum-seller, who cruelly and remorselessly plies his wicked trade to the undoing of his fellow beings.

Now there is not a young man who has reached the age of intelligent accountability, who does not know that the indulgence in intoxicating drinks is the sure road to ruin. There is not an habitual drinker or drunkard who does not realize that he is "sowing to the wind," and that erelong he will "reap the whirlwind"—that he is feeding his brain with a subtile poison that is slowly but surely sapping the foundations of reason, judgment, will,—that he is courting physical decay and death for himself, and poverty and wretchedness for his family. There is not one of all this class, who, in yielding himself to the demon habit of drink, does not do so of his own enlightened volition, thereby advertising himself to the world as one incompetent to withstand the temptations of life, and who, unless he reforms, the sooner he drinks himself to death the better it will be for his family and friends.

The world wants men who can walk unscathed through the flames of hell, if necessary, and with no trace of smoke clinging to their garments. Certain it is it has but little use for those who yield themselves willing victims to soul-destroying habits whose evils are placarded upon the rum-blossomed visages, battered forms, wrecked lives and ruined homes they witness all around them. How is it to obtain this better order of humanity? Certainly not by wasting much sympathy upon drunkards. Pity it is, rather, that alcoholic poisons were not more deadly in their effects, that they might operate more quickly in ridding the world of those who

have no more manhood than to yield themselves willing victims to their baneful influence.

There are enough people in the world, for
all practical purposes, who do not need this
eternal preaching against intemperance.
Their heads are level against the demoral-
izing vices and dissipations of life. They
are the only kind the world needs. The
rest can be better spared than not.

We do not believe intemperance can ever
be made sufficiently odious to deter men
from becoming sots until the odium of the
liquor traffic is shifted from the rum-seller to
the rum-drinker. Inebriation should be made
such a stigma and shame—such a brand of
infamy—that men would shun it as they
would the plague. Young women should
refuse to associate with young men who use
intoxicating liquor. And as to marrying
one of that class—an habitual drinker,—they
had better take to their arms a putrifying
corpse, reeking with the foul odors of the
grave. Drunkenness should be made justifiable grounds for divorce ; and wives should
refuse to bear children to drunken husbands.
The habitual drunkard should be disfran-

chised as one unfit to exercise the rights of citizenship. Drunkenness should be regarded as a brand of weakness—of an effeminate and worthless manhood to be hated and loathed of all the earth.

A little of this sort of treatment, it strikes us, would go further in the way of temperance reform than all the invective that can possibly be heaped upon the heads of the liquor-sellers.

PROVIDENCE seldom troubles Himself much about the welfare of a man who does not put forth every effort in his power to take care of himself. And yet He no doubt has a cordial hatred for the one who makes his own welfare the exclusive aim and end of existence.

THE man who thinks in the groove marked out for him to think in, should have the manliness to get out of his groove long enough to respect the one who strikes out in new paths, and thinks for himself even though the latter should think erroneously.

INSPIRATION OF GOOD DEEDS.

ONE of our noblest and purest-souled women writes: "I never read of a noble act that it does not inspire me to something higher. I never read and study meanness and hypocrisy that it does not fill me with a deeper loathing and despising for that which is low in life." And so our acts, whether of good or evil, are made helps to the better life of all true souls. No one can live wholly for himself. His influence in some way reaches out and takes in all humanity. If for good, then all are in some manner made better thereby. If for evil, then will it be wholly evil only to himself? All glory and honor to the man or woman who lives to inspire others to "something higher."

THE man who does not grow wiser and better as he grows older, has no business to be here ; and the sooner death catches him out, the better for the world.

THE man or woman who can not find sweet companionship and profitable society in his or her own soul is poorly qualified for companionship with other souls. The miser who counts over his treasures wants no companion to share the satisfaction he feels. He finds a sordid joy in solitude. The soul enriched with the treasures of knowledge, and the heart schooled in the virtues that ennoble and beautify human character, is never companionless. Its treasures are a well-spring of never failing joy. It never wearies of conning them o'er and o'er. Time never hangs heavily on its hands. It is never lonesome, nor troubled with that haunting demon of empty brains, *ennui*.

Some good people of culture and large intelligence have an idea that it is necessary always to *entertain* their friends. We concede that such entertainment is expected and is actually necessary to the happiness of a large class of the human family; but we should pray for deliverance from all such friends. Not that we would be understood as intimating that in association we may not find true enjoyment, nor that the attrition of thought—of mind with mind—is not essential in bringing out sterling traits of character, and the finest intellectual qualities ; but the idea we would convey is one of self-reliance. Make friends with yourself—fill the chambers of your soul with delightful companions, and no trouble can come to you, or losses befall you, that will leave you wholly forsaken. You will then have resources of enjoyment to fall back upon that no legal process can deprive you of—intellectual and spiritual treasures beyond the jurisdiction of the courts—a bank account that can not be overdrawn.

The emptiest thing in all this world is an empty soul ; and whoever is content to sit down with folded hands in quiet indifference, amid all the unappropriated riches of the universe—the golden stores of thought—the unexplored caves of knowledge,—and live on and on in emptiness, satisfied with his spiritual and intellectual poverty, has no right to intrude his idleness and worthlessness upon the precious moments of men and women who have no time to waste.

But whoever has an aspiration for better things—would seek to ascend the shining hights and realize the fruition that awaits his efforts—will never want for a helping hand to assist him on the way. All true souls are ever delighted to help and encourage others ; but they should never be taxed to waste their strength on those who make no effort to help themselves.

He is not wise who counts himself poor simply because he possesses but a humble store of this world's goods ; for what are houses and lands, and a few shining baubles of earth, to the vast treasures of the universe that are the common heritage of all aspiring souls ?

It is far more creditable for a young lady to earn her own livelihood by some respectable vocation, than to marry some rich fool for the sake of a home.

THE RELIGION OF LAUGHTER.

THE Creator of man is also the Creator of monkeys. He who implanted the spirit of mirth in human nature also put the warble in the throat of the canary, the grimace on the face of the baboon, and the pucker in the persimmon. Nature is ever inviting to wholesome recreation and diversion.

A world with a sky eternally overcast with clouds, with never a rift of sunshine— never a cloud with a silver lining—would be a most gloomy place of abode. And yet there are people who seem to think that sunshine is a curse ; that a hearty laugh is sure evidence of total depravity. Tears, sighs and groans, with a lugubrious expression of countenance that would start the goose-pimples on the back of any fun-loving Christian, is their normal condition—their idea of true religion.

Of such were the old, unsavory misanthropes and pious lazzaroni who abjured all the comforts and pleasures of life, and mor-

tified their worthless bodies with all manner
of deprivations, and even tortures, under
the mistaken idea that they were thereby
serving their Master. Of such, also, evidently, is the editor of the New York
Evangelist, who regards all mirth as sinful,
and who fortifies his argument with such
nonsense as this : " In the record of the life
of Christ on earth we have no intimation
that He ever indulged in laughter. Not one
of the Prophets or Apostles ever attempted
the exercise of wit in their writings. Nor is
there anything in the description of Heaven
to lead us to suppose that laughter is indulged in there."

If the saints in Heaven never laugh—if
they are never permitted to indulge in the
least bit of innocent fun, but must go around
forever in a chronic condition of psalm-sing-
ing sadness—we don't want to go there. We
would prefer to take our lot with the frolick-
ing kids.

Seriously, we believe in the religion of fun
—not of perpetual frivolity and nonsense,
but of rational recreation and enjoyment—a
religion that can " weep with them that

weep, and rejoice with those that rejoice ;" a religion that delights to bask in the sunshine, and would help to dispel the clouds and gloom that lower over the world.

Trouble and sorrow come to all. There are vastly more aching hearts in the world than appears upon the surface. Many a hidden grief is glossed over with a smile.

What millions of souls need most of all is the leaven of a cheerful, abiding trust—a reconciliation with the universe. They need the warm pressure of a cheerful, loving hand, to lead them out of the darkness and gloom of their own morbid, inharmonious natures, and into the gladsome sunlight and good cheer of a laughter-loving existence.

THE man who thinks it no wrong to defraud the State,—either by evading the payment of his just proportion of taxes, or by receiving from the government what is not justly his due,—possesses all the elements of a first-class thief. He needs but time and opportunity to develop a high order of faculty for highway robbery.

IT does no good to rail at the world—to blame and condemn everybody, who does not exactly come up to our idea of what they should be—who does not think as we think, and could not by any possibility, unless possessed of exactly the same shape and quality of brain, and had been born and reared under exactly the same conditions. The head might as well rail at the hand for any infirmity the latter may possess, or the hand find fault with the foot for like reason. We are all members of one social body, and common sense should teach us that scolding, or harsh measures of any sort only aggravate the evils that we seek to correct.

When we have a broken limb we procure the services of a surgeon, the bones are carefully adjusted and held in place, and the wound tenderly nursed, until nature effects a cure. The limb is sometimes so badly injured that amputation is necessary to preserve the rest of the body. Society is instituted on very much the same principle as the human body. There are heads to do the thinking, shoulders to bear the burdens, hands to perform the labor and stomachs to consume the fruits of labor,—and the latter often without giving an equivalent in return.

Wrong doers exist everywhere. They are the broken limbs, the bunions and carbuncles, the goiter and fever sores, the torpid livers and stomach-aches of society. They can't all be amputated or dissected. If they could be, and were, there would be but precious little of the body left. It would be but a dismantled hulk, with some staunch timbers and sound planks, but the whole badly sprung and liable to fall in pieces of its own weight.

How best to cure the infirmities of society has been the problem of the ages. The regular doctors have had the patient in charge for nearly two thousand years, but with only indifferent success. It has been salivated, blistered and physicked until it has come to have a deep-seated disgust for all sorts of moral nostrums ; and in some instances has taken to quackery with still worse results, or to no medicine at all, and perhaps died a natural and spiritual death.

Now, what the world needs most is that better knowledge which teaches the great principle of kindness as a rule of action in the treatment of the frailties, imperfections and moral infirmities of the race. The cure must commence with the individual and radiate outward like the warmth of the sunshine, or the glow and glory of a manly soul. It is man's truest and noblest mission to nurse the weak, reprove with gentleness the wayward, strengthen and encourage the faltering and console the sorrowing ; and thereby, if possible, to leave the world better than he found it. If he succeed in making his own life sweet and unselfish he will have accomplished much. If he learn the laws of physical health and faithfully obey them, his simple example will be a light to the path of others which will not be lost to the world, and if in the spirit of that broad humanity and charity that recognizes kinship in all, and sees good in all, he seeks the highest welfare of his brother man,—one such life will be worth more to the world than vast volumes of moral essays frigid with thought but barren of heart-throbs.

Let us learn this lesson, that a selfish life is a mean life, and that the good we do to others reacts upon ourselves in the formation . and building up of a character that will constitute the only wealth we can ever carry with us into the land of the Beyond.

A TRUE GENTLEMAN,

A TRUE gentleman is a rarer thing among men than many suppose. It isn't wealth, nor fine clothes, nor much learning, nor high social position, that always indicate a real gentleman. He is quite as apt to be found in the absence of all these advantages and accomplishments, as otherwise. The principle of true gentility is a difficult . thing to be acquired ; it must be inbred in the heart to be lasting and reliable. No gentleman ever intentionally wounds the feelings of another without cause. He is never rude, or coarse, or impolite. He is always the true and chivalrous friend of woman, defending her honor and good name whenever and wherever assailed. He never by word or act calls the blush of offended modesty to the cheek of innocent girlhood. Children, meeting him alone, look up with trustful confidence into his face. He has always a kind word for a fellow being in distress, and a helping hand for the needy. He is never discourteous or overbearing to his inferiors, nor disrespectful to his superiors. What he does not know he wisely contents himself to wait and learn. He judges others by the standard of genuine character, rather than by any factitious circumstance of wealth and surroundings. He is a friend that may be trusted, and would scorn to betray an enemy. He never gossips, nor repeats scandalous stories of his neighbors. He prefers to think kindly and charitably of all. In short he is a gentleman.

THE man or woman who gives expression to a thought calculated to benefit or bless mankind, is deserving of honor in this world, and a place in the affections of angels.

LIFE'S TEMPLE.

I STOOD by the mystical altar
    Of my wondering, worshiping soul ;
While out from my being's deep center,
    O'er-arching and crowning the whole,
A temple in majesty lifted
    Its dome like an infinite scroll.

With columns of marvelous whiteness
    And patterns of strangest design ;
Its wall wrought of purple and crimson,
    All cunning and beauty combine ;
And here by the soul's silent altar
    I stood—in this temple of mine.

'Twas morn, and the scintillant splendor
    Of BEING flashed over my way,
Like the tide of the orient sunbeams
    Rushing in to embrace the new day—
Enfolding the earth in its glory,
    And driving the shadows away.

Around me were groups of strange faces,
    And forms that intruded between
The light that streamed in at the windows,
    And flooded with dazzling sheen
The altar, whereon there were written
    Life's lessons, all plain to be seen.

The faces were those of the demons
    Of evil, that lurk to betray—
Of Pride and of selfish Ambition—
    Of indolence—eager to lay
Their snares for the feet of my spirit
    While traversing life's rugged way.

And yet did they seem to my vision
    Transfigured to angels of light—
Fair tempters, of ravishing beauty,
    Beguiling to gentle delight ;
As the rose-tinted glow of the sunset
    Entices to darkness and night.

Then I turned me away from the altar,
    With its lessons of Truth, for awhile
To list to the voice of their pleading,
    And dwell in the light of a smile
That was cruel, and cold, and false-hearted—
    That lured evermore to beguile.

    *   *   *   *

And ever the altar remaineth
    Emblazoned in letters of gold,
To lighten the pathway of duty
    To pleasures of being untold—
All time and the mighty hereafter
    Its teachings forever enfold.

LIFE is too short to waste any one of its
golden moments in anger.

THERE are many people who are egotistical enough to imagine that if they had had the making of the Universe they could have improved somewhat on the present job. They would have had no conjunction of the planets, nor great disturbances of Nature of any kind—no pestilence nor drought—no tidal waves nor tornadoes—no sickness nor sorrow—none of the ills or calamities that flesh is heir to. They would have made the earth ever fruitful, the elements ever propitious, and life ever fair and prosperous.

But is it not probable that under such conditions humanity would have been about as tame and insipid as the life of a jelly fish? As the thunder storm clears and purifies the atmosphere, as the furnace fires burn away the dross, so man's struggle with the elements is necessary to build up his individuality and round out his character. He must needs wrestle with the pestilence and the storm —with Summer's heat and Winter's cold—

with health and life-destroying elements—
with the hard conditions of existence that
meet him at every turn. His struggles give
him strength and vigor of limb and soul, and
enable him to walk erect where otherwise he
would shrivel back into the primitive type of
being whence he sprung.

Man's business here is to deal with the
Universe as he finds it, and to adjust himself
to it in every possible way ; not to quarrel
with it. Nature takes no more thought of
him as a physical being than she does of the
reptile or the rock. Law is as merciless as
the glacier. Upon its crest is safety—harmony. Beneath it, grinding atoms. Whoever violates the laws of health or being,
intentionally or ignorantly, suffers—dies. He
must bear the pain until Nature, gentle
mother, soothes the sufferer to rest. There
is no vicarious atonement for matter.
Though the mother love be never so strong
it can not avert the mortal agony of the
darling child.

Nature every where and always commands
implicit obedience to her laws. She will
have it at any cost ; and the sooner man

learns this fact, and profits by it, the better
will it be for him.   He should learn a lesson
of the reed, that bends before the storm ; of
the lichen, that anchors itself to the rock ; of
the flower, that lifts its head in the sunshine ;
of the bird, that carols among the branches ;
of the bat, that hides in the cave by day ; of
the laughter of children, and the heart-throbs
of sorrow ; of the earthquake and the lightning ; of plenty and famine ; of health and
sickness ; of birth and death.   Nature will
deal kindly with him if he will but obey her.
She will gladden his life with blessings in a
thousand ways.   She will croon to him in
the ripple of her brooks, and in the murmur
of her ocean waves.   She will fan him with
her zephyrs ladened with the fragrance of
many flowers.   She will give him health of
body and cheerfulness of soul.   She will
bend over him her loving skies all radient
with stars, and will beckon him onward and
upward to higher planes of being.   ,

The grandest thing in the Universe, of
which we have any knowledge, is a noble
soul, living to some noble end.   This is Nature's crowning fruition—her rarest handi-

work. To be noble and live nobly should be the aim and ambition of all. In such lives we behold the promise and prophecy of a yet to be glorious humanity.

SUNDAY.

IT was Sancho Panza, we believe, the factotum and servant of the Knight of the Rueful Countenance, who gave utterance to the memorable saying, "Blessed be the man that invented sleep." We might supplement the saying, or move as an amendment, "Blessed be the man that invented Sunday."

Looked upon simply as a human institution —and in that light we are disposed to regard it—it is the very embodiment of human wisdom. Indeed it is the grandest of all inventions—one fraught with the greatest consequences to the race. It is the sunburst through the cloud—the light upon the tower —the gleam of hope and joy to the soul.

To all mankind work of some sort is a necessity. To the vast majority it is the weary bearing of heavy and often times painful burdens, with no rest nor respite save that which comes of the precious custom which dedicates and, in a religious sense, consecrates one-seventh of the time to rest. Although Sunday is claimed by the church as a holy day, to be devoted exclusively to religious uses, it also belongs to the world to be enjoyed as reason and conscience should ever dictate. It was made for man, and is the property of all who claim it. "Let no man therefore," says Paul, "judge you in meat, or in drink, or in respect of an holy-day, or of the new moon, or of the Sabbath days."

A healthy public sentiment needs no Sunday law to enforce a general observance of the day. By making Sunday a non-judicial day, wherein no civil business is required to be performed, the State acts most wisely. In this it has the approval of every citizen ; and in this also it invites a general suspension of business, that, as far as possible, all may enjoy the rest they need.

To secure the best and truest blessings of Sunday it is found necessary that a few should work in order to enhance the comfort and enjoyment of the many. Take, for instance, the ferries and trains leading from our great cities, upon the only day wherein the toiling multitudes can escape for a breath of fresh air, or a baptism of God's beautiful sunshine. Take our religious teachers, who are required to perform their hardest work on Sunday ; our hotel and house-keepers also, and many others, who can not escape the necessity of toil upon that day. Surely some must work for others to profit and enjoy. There is no reasonable escape from it.

What society wants is a higher appreciation of the privileges of Sunday. But more than all it wants an order of humanity that will have a higher appreciation of all days, and of the opportunities of life generally. It can not well have the former until it secures the latter. All that hurts or degrades man, physically or spiritually ; all that retards his moral and intellectual advancement ; in short, all that is not a help to him in some way, should be discountenanced. To this end every good citizen should lend a helping hand. For in that direction lies the truest welfare of society.

Then, "welcome, sweet day of rest." Welcome, thrice welcome, to the world's weary ones weighed down with the burdens of many cares. How glad the solace that comes of a day of rest to the tired hand and exhausted brain. Eternal Spirit of Wisdom, Love and Truth, give us to choose the better way of life .that shall lead up to a Sabbath day of eternal rest and peace.

HE who strives and fails should never despair. He should look within and start anew—take honor for his chart, courage for his compass, and the highest moral and mental culture for the point he would reach, —then there will be, there can be, "no such word as fail."

POVERTY and riches are only relative terms. They are to a large extent figments of the brain—creatures of the imagination. He only is poor who thinks himself so ; and no one is truly rich who is not rich in soul.

THE great curse of the age, with our young men, is their persistent attempts to live a fifteen-or-twenty-dollars-a-week style of life on a ten-or-twelve-dollars income. The problem is just about as difficult of solution as that of the passage of two railroad trains in opposite directions over the same track.

Now, while we fully appreciate the natural aversion that the average young man has to being lectured at, yet we apprehend that a few friendly hints and suggestions, offered in a spirit of sympathy for him and charity for his mistakes, will not be taken amiss.

We fully understand the nature of the temptations with which our young men are constantly beset. Naturally sociable and disposed to be convivial, they find their enjoyment mainly in association. They meet upon the street corners, and at the saloons; they find a hundred avenues for their somewhat limited means. (We refer to clerks and mechanics who earn all the way from fifty to a hundred dollars a month.) They treat each other to cigars and beer, play billiards, euchre, and occasionally a game of draw poker, and thus they readily run through from five to ten dollars a night, perhaps more ; and find themselves "dead broke" and in debt at the end of the week.

By far the most deceptive and dangerous of all the vices to which our young men are exposed is that of gambling, for it carries with it nearly every other vice in the dark catalogue. Especially does it go hand in hand with drinking ; and, if persisted in, will as surely lead to ruin as the needle points to the pole.

In every populous community there can be found a number of well-dressed, genial, hale fellows, who seem to have no fixed occupation. They spend their nights in manipulating the cards, and are up to all the tricks of their trade which come of skill and long practice. These men live mainly off our young mechanics and clerks, who foolishly imagine they can cope with them in their especial vocation.

And then there is another class of young men, who manage somehow to dress well and hold up their heads in society, who attend all the sociables and parties, and are occasionally seen riding after a spanking team. "They toil not, neither do they spin." It is said of them that "they never miss a meal nor spend a cent." They are what Beecher would call a species of parasite. They live by borrowing. They meet our industrious young men at every turn. They know when pay day comes, the exact amount that each of their friends receives, and are promptly on hand to strike them for a " piece."

Any young man who is in the habit of spending his evenings "up town," knows all about these, and various other kinds of parasites. He realizes that if his earnings were double what they are he would not be able to meet all the demands and drains made upon him.

But what is he to do? Would you deprive him of all social pleasure—of all enjoyment of friendly intercourse with his companions and fellows? Not at all ; we would elevate the standard and character of his enjoyments. Instead of his indulging in those practices which destroy health and debase the soul, we would inspire him with a taste for those enjoyments which ennoble the man—which add health and length of years—which adorn and beautify for time and eternity.

See here, my boy, do you know the real enjoyment there is in a good book? Are you familiar with our standard authors? Have you read Dickens and Washington Irving? Has your mind ever caught the glow and glory that flash out from the works of those great thinkers of the age, Huxley, Lecky, Herbert Spencer, Tyndall, Darwin, John Stuart Mill, and others? Do you know what real and unfading joy there is in the companionship of good books? Compared with the soul-destroying pleasures of a night's carouse, they are as daylight to the murky night—the calm of a Spring morning to the dismal wail of the tempest. Suppose you "turn over a new leaf" for a while, and try it. Shake off some of the leeches that are sucking your life out. Provide yourself with some choice books and spend your evenings at home. Deposit five dollars of your weekly earnings in a savings bank. Try it for a year ; and our word for it, at the end of that period you will find yourself, in addition to the money saved, in possession of a stock of manhood, self-respect and general knowledge that will be worth to you a thousand times the effort it costs.

EVIL HABITS.

THE power of evil habit is almost as strong as Nature itself. Indeed, it becomes "second nature," when its hold upon one is not easily broken—just as an excrescence upon a tree becomes, from growth, a part of the tree itself.

Character is made up of an aggregation of habits,—good, bad and indifferent. Hence, the importance, to young people especially, of forming as many of the former, and as few of the bad and indifferent as possible.

The young man who yields himself a slave

to any debasing habit, mortgages his body to corruption and his soul to the Devil (if there be a Devil). His manhood must indeed be of an inferior quality if, while revolting at his chains, he nevertheless lacks the power to break them.

But we do not believe in that kind of absolute subjection to habit. We believe it possible, by a proper exercise of will, for any sane person to throw off the shackles of evil habit, and go forth into the world a free man. We are free agents to that extent that we certainly have command of our own bodies. We can surely eat or drink that which pollutes or destroys, or we can leave it alone. We can keep ourselves wholesome and clean, or we can wallow in all manner of impurity.

We insist that no person who permits himself to associate with his fellows, or who thrusts himself into their presence, has the moral right to offend his associates by his personal untidiness. He has no moral right to poison the atmosphere which others are compelled to breathe with the vile odors of tobacco or rum.

There are many otherwise excellent people who are so abjectly the slaves of these twin habits of evil that they will tell you they have not the power to break loose from them. We do not believe them. We do not believe the man lives, with brains enough to know that he is a man, who can not, if he will, rise superior to all evil habits—who can not turn away from all that defiles the temple of the living soul, and walk henceforth in an atmosphere of physical purity.

A wise man will learn from, and profit by experience. Whatever he finds hurtful to his physical health he will school himself to abjure, no matter how great the temporary gratification therefrom. If he does not find the indulgence in any habit really hurtful, he will ask himself the questions, What good does it bring me? Does it make me a more wholesome companion for the one whose lot is cast by my side? Is the cost one that I can readily afford? and could I not use the money to a better purpose?

If that pale, effeminate young man at the street corner, who has acquired the modern scholastic art of deftly rolling a cigarette, and who can expel the smoke therefrom through his nose, without the least sympathetic moisture of the eye, could only realize the enervating effect upon his physical system—that he is pickling the nerves and tissues of his body with a subtile poison that will make him a walking stench among men and angels—it would seem that he would "swear off" forever.

This is a hard world to wrestle with at best. One needs all his powers of mind and body—perfect health of brain and brawn—to stand up manfully in the front rank and do brave work. He who fritters away his strength by indulgence in any debasing habit, is fitting himself to take a back seat in the drama of life. He is making of himself a donkey for others to ride.

Young man, break the fetters of evil habit, and stand forth in the freedom of a noble and unsullied manhood, with your face to the front. Strong of will and panoplied with good resolutions, go forth to noble conquests, the garnered fruits of which shall constitute treasures of soul that "nor moth

nor rust can corrupt, nor thieves break through
and steal."

MUSINGS,

THERE are souls in the magnitude of
whose grand, divine natures, all goodness and nobility of character seem to be
gathered—souls whom but to know is to
reverence and adore. Not upon thrones, or
in the high places of earth, need we look for
them, for there they are seldom to be found ;
but in the humbler walks of life, and in the
silent ways of duty, we may behold them,
shining out like diamonds among the common
things of earth. But who can fathom the
intensity of such natures ! Indeed, what a
restless, longing torturing thing is a finely
organized, sensitive human nature. Born to
suffering and to joy, how keen to every
emotion of sorrow or of pleasure. To-day
radiant with the sunlight that plays on the
mountain peaks of heaven—to-morrow a bird
with broken wing hiding amid the shadows.
—So keyed to the divine harmonies—so

sensitive to the discords and jarrings of social
life—that existence becomes at times almost
intolerable. Others there are who live so
completely in the physical that they need
but to be well fed and well sheltered to be
happy. But it is the happiness of the sloth
basking in the sun—of the insensate lichen
vegetating upon the rock. The soul's capacity for enjoyment is measured by its
power to suffer. Hence it is an open question with some whether the higher life of the
soul is at all desirable, for with it must ever
come the unsatisfied outreachings of the
deathless spirit—its quenchless thirst for
" more." And yet infinitely better this than
the life of the mollusk—of the dull clod, that
lives its little day, and dies, "thrust foully
into earth to be forgot." Better the night of
storm and darkness, followed by the rose-
tinted daybreak and the glorious morn, than
the continuous glare of a never setting sun.
Better the keen agony with its vivid compensation of gladness, than the life whose
heart-throb never leaps with the lightning of
passion, nor quivers with the emotion of
tender sympathy.

SOPHISTRIES.

I N an article by an eminent physician in the *New England Medical Journal* we find these somewhat startling assertions : " Insane people, like those who are sane, " have no power to resist the strongest mo- " tive. No beings that ever lived possessed " the power to do different from what they " did."

There is a sophistry of reasoning calcu- lated to mislead and befog the mind. By it wrong may be made to appear right, light darkness. Such we. regard the reasoning that leads the mind to such conclusions as those given above.

For instance, we are told by those who believe in this irresponsibility of action that no sane mind acts without motive—that mo- tive is not subject to will—that the mind must necessarily yield to the strongest motive,— and that therefore whatever a man does he is compelled to do.

This process of reasoning, if accepted,

leaves the opponents of such conclusions without any ground to stand on. It takes away from man the last vestige of moral accountability, and makes him the veriest shuttlecock of irresistible fate.

If such was the prevailing belief of the world, man would soon settle back into the lower types of life whence he sprung, and chaos would come again. But the reasoning, in our judgment, is fallacious, and the conclusions wrong.

It is no doubt true that man is very largely subject to conditions of birth, education and surroundings. We can readily see that he is a free moral agent only in a limited sense, if at all. If born in vice, and educated in crime, he will be very apt to be a criminal—although the rule is not absolutely invariable ; and it is this variation of rule that lies at the basis of all evolution. Like a horse tethered to a stake, with freedom to crop the herbage over a circumscribed area, so man, in a moral sense, is free to act within a certain length of rope. He knows the right from the wrong. He is capable of weighing and determining the motives that prompt him to do the one or avoid the other. If the wrong he does was the right . thing for him to do,—the thing concerning which he had no volition and was compelled to do—why should he experience regret for wrong doing?

We say the reasoning which leads to such fatal conclusions as those quoted is erroneous. It makes man a mere machine, as helpless as the weather vane upon a church steeple, or the insensate clod that is swept along by the flood.

The man who acts upon a criminal impulse or motive to steal, where detection and punishment are uncertain, restrains that impulse with the certainty of detection and punishment before him. Thus he is able to shape and control motive. And just here the weak point in the reasoning referred to is seen to be that it is based upon false premises. The strongest motive is not irresistible ; or, if it is, then it is in some sense subject to the will. That is, one who wants a plausible excuse for doing wrong can readily shape the motive to afford him that excuse.

The human intellect is as many sided as

the shapes of the brain. In its operations we find that there is a mysterious something that seems to sit behind all the faculties, and that stimulates or curbs their actions—that encourages this and condemns that. This is the EGO—the conscious ME—the autocrat of volition. Otherwise there could be no such thing as reason or judgment.

No man ever lived that did his best in all directions of his nature. If he reasoned himself into the conviction that he did, it was simply that he might find a pretext for doing something that his inclinations invited, but which his judgment condemned.

Once grounded in this fatalism there would be nothing to stimulate man to effort. Why should he try, when trying costs self-denial and toil, and oftentimes sore hardship and privation? It would be far easier not to try. Why should he walk the thorny path of duty when the way of indolent ease was far more inviting? Besides, he would be entitled to no credit therefor. If he went to the bad he couldn't help it, and if he did not it would be all the same! It is well for the world that men reject such conclusions.

———

"KEEP to the right," is a law of the road, which, when obeyed, saves one a world of trouble.

Society is a public highway on a grand scale—a great moral turnpike whereon a hurrrying, jostling, restless crowd of badly assorted humanity is ever thronging. Here is life in all its better phases—childhood with its golden hair and wondering eyes; youth with its widening, thoughtful outlook; manhood with its firm step and earnest purpose; old age with its bowed form and whitened locks. Here, too, are thickly strewn the wrecks of life—misguided childhood, headstrong and wayward; erring youth, rioting in frivolity and dissipation, and sowing the seeds of physical decay and moral death; vicious manhood, treading the downward road; and decrepit age, sinister and sere, with its painful memories, and hopeless future,—all commingling in the one great journey from the cradle to the grave.

How much discord, inharmony and jostling would be avoided, in this journey, if each traveler would only "keep to the right."

There is a pitfall before you, young man—a temptation to evil—a snare for your feet. You are forming habits of idleness, dissipation and extravagance, which will stick to you like the shirt of Nessus, hampering your nobler efforts, and eventually dragging you down to the gateway of despair. Keep to the right and avoid it.

That is a doubtful business venture, sir, in which you are about to engage,—one, perhaps, involving loss of self-respect and sacrifice of manly principle. You see where, by taking advantage of your neighbor's ignorance, you can get the best of him in a trade ; or by some smart trick of the law you can evade some responsibility you have willingly assumed, or shirk some duty that lies in your way. Keep to the right ; there only is the path of honor.

You, neighbor, when tempted to deal in gossip or scandal,—to give way to the natural meanness within you—to let your temper get the upper hand of your judgment

—to play the tyrant in your family—to withhold the gentle word of love or praise from her who walks by your side—to lower the standard of your honor, or do ought that would make you less manly or noble in the eyes of good men or angels, keep to the right.

"Keep to the right." These golden words should be engraven in letters of living light on the temple of every human soul. They should stand forth as finger-posts at the junction of every wrong—at the point of every divergence from the straight path of rectitude—by every wayside temptation. Keep to the right, young man, spurning every ignoble thought—every unmanly action. Thus will you lay up treasures for a grand old age, and life will bear for you its richest fruits.

PARENTS who wear out their lives in the acquisition of property to leave for their children to scatter, do a double wrong— first to themselves and next to their children. The bird that would learn to fly must lean on its own wings.

CRAB-APPLE DIGNITY,

SOME people are got up on the crab-apple plan. They are so sour and puckery that no one cares to pluck them. Whoever attempted it would be apt to prick his fingers with the thorns and wish he had not undertaken the job. They seem to enjoy themselves most when they are most miserable. They are constantly on the look-out for slights and affronts, and live in a chronic condition of apprehensiveness that somebody will say something about them they may not hear. They pride themselves on their bluntness, and glory in their angularities. They are the moral porcupines of society, whom it were better not to disturb, but to turn out for and pass on the other side. Such people little realize how much of the real enjoyments of life they miss—how much they withhold from their fellows.

It surely pays to be affable, especially as it costs nothing. It requires no more effort of the vocal organs to speak kindly than unkindly, and generally not as much. We can scatter flowers or brambles in our pathway— sunshine or shade. Who would not greatly prefer the former to the latter?

Social and domestic life would be infinitely sweeter if people generally cultivated the suavities and tried to make themselves agreeable. Some people imagine they are dignified, when in fact they are only morose and cross-grained. They walk through life with the solemnity of an owl, surrounded by an atmosphere as crisp and frosty as the breath of an iceberg. In the home circle, in social life, in the walks of business, their presence is enough to start the "goose pimples" upon the back of every person with a sunny nature. Such people may have their uses in the world, but we have never been able to discover exactly wherein.

Give us for companionship the man or woman with as little of that kind of dignity as possible—one that can romp with child-hood—can laugh with those who laugh and weep with those who weep. Give us the man or woman with nature all radiant with the glow and gladness of a sympathetic humanity—one that never mistakes indigestion for religion, or a torpid liver for sobriety. There are, thank goodness, many such in the world. If there were not we should lose faith in the race, and believe no more in the law of human progress. The millennium would be but a wild fantasy of the imagination—a never-to-be realized dream.

It is in the goodness, the nobility, of the few that we behold the prophecy of better things for all. Hence, we take courage and move on, content to labor and to wait—to plant the seed and bide the fruitage.

Few people strive to do their best—none fully succeed. The heroism is in the striving. If all would try, the world would be the better for it. But some are so constituted that they have little or no disposition to try. What we want is a breed of humanity that has the deeply-rooted determination to climb to a better life and the grip to hold on. It will come some time, we believe, in the march of the ages.

A BORN rogue is the hardest kind of a rogue to reform.

HERE are no hearts so brave or strong that do not at times quail before some great sorrow. The shadow falls across their pathway when they are least expecting it, or least prepared for it, shutting out the bright sky and beautiful sunshine, and not even leaving one star to beckon them away to brighter realms. Suddenly spreads the pall of gloom over the soul, like the dark and remorseless hand of fate, and where so lately was heard the music and melody of the spheres—the laughter of children, the songs of birds and the sweet voice of love—is heard the wail of woe, or keen anguish riots in silence among the heartstrings. Death lays its icy finger upon the lips we love—the heart that nestled close to ours through the golden days of our lives is torn from our arms for aye—the voice that made sweet melody in our ears is heard no more—and the agony, keen and pitiless, is upon us like an avalanche ere we are aware.

We say, these shadows come to all.
They are incident to this mortal life. It
could not well be otherwise in this earthly
stage of existence. Men may preach till the
"crack of doom" the philosophies that
should reconcile us to these great over-
whelming sorrows. Such preaching is always
for others, not for ourselves. When our
own hearts are riven—when the arrow pierces
our own souls—we must enter the Gethse-
mane of anguish alone. There is none to
bear our burdens, no more than there was to
bear the burdens of Him, the Man of Sorrows, in that agonizing struggle wherein we
are told He "sweat great drops of blood."

But Nature, gentle mother, although
seemingly cruel as the grave, is nevertheless
tender and kind. Over the field of carnage
and death, where shot and shell plow their
way through struggling masses of living men,
and the earth is rent and torn, and made
ghastly with the mangled slain, the dews
and the gentle rains descend like a bene-
diction, and over all the balm of the sunshine, like the smile of God, sheds its sweet
baptism, and erelong the grasses and the

wild flowers come with their soft and beautiful vestments to hide the cruel scars of war.
So with the stricken heart. In time the fury
of the storm is spent ; the tempest and the
whirlwind of emotion are lulled to sleep, and
rest and peace, with their mild and gentle
solace, come with angel fingers to bind up
the bruised heart and calm the troubled soul.

These are the experiences of life that
come to all. They are the experiences that
seem most necessary to discipline the soul
and fit it for that higher plane of life and
usefulness, towards which all progressed and
progressive humanity is tending.

The lesson we would draw from this
theme is, that while we can not avert these
apparently dire events in our lives, we should
school our natures to accept them as a part
of the training and discipline we need, and
without which we should be but poorly qualified for those higher spiritual and intellectual
enjoyments to which, whether ever to be
realized or not, every true soul should aspire.
We should learn to feel that they are the
refining fires that burn away the dross and
coarseness of our natures—that they are

stepping-stones, if rightly used, to a higher plane of thought and feeling.

PASSING ON,

IN the great sum of human life of how little significance is each individual unit. Even the world's greatest men and women drop out of the places they once occupied, and which we thought no others could fill as well, and are soon forgotten ; or, if they live, it is in their works rather than in their individual memories. Thus Homer, Shakspere, Milton, Byron, Titian, Mozart, and all the world's once great masters of song and art, are no longer personal entities to us ; but rather the works which they wrought, and in which they will live forever.

In the state, in communities, in the smaller circles of public, social and domestic life, our best known citizens, friends and neighbors, one after another, pass away,—a moment's surprise, a sigh of tender regret, a heart-burst of agony, perhaps,—and soon no trace or ripple is left upon the surface of life's broad sea. In public life, or in the ranks of citizenship, their places are soon filled by others, the dismembered ranks are closed, and the onward march is unbroken forever.

Of all the world's countless millions, sweeping onward in vast cycles from infancy to old age, how few are remembered longer than during the generation in which they live. Like the shifting colors of the kaleido-scope, such is human life—ever changing into new and wonderful forms ; and ever evolving from the lower forms types of the higher, and the higher still, to mark the steadily advancing progress of the race.

Death and decay is written upon all life. He through whose veins now flows the red tide of health, whose will is strong to do and dare, and whose hand is quick to perform, nurses in his bosom the seeds of dissolution, which will ere long bourgeon and blossom, and bear fruit for the grave. The cheek and eye of beauty, that glow to-day with the sparkle of roseate health, will wither and pale with age, or fade away at the touch of disease and death.

Thus, even in man's proudest and best estate, how absolutely little does he not seem. How vain his unbridled ambitions—how empty the laurels the world places on his brow. A few years hence and naught of himself will remain but a handful of dust that a breath would scatter into nothingness. The good or evil that he did—the deeds that he wrought—are all that will survive to bless or tarnish his memory.

This, then, should be the end and aim of all, to so act that this life shall not not only afford to each its largest meed of health and happiness, but that the memory of things done—the monuments of good deeds erected here—shall survive the mutations of time, to blaze the way for others who are to follow.

HE who is a stockholder in the stars, in the glad sunshine, in the fragrance of the flowers, in the songs of birds and in the laughter of children, and who has an interest in the aspirations and outreachings of humanity, is the possessor of treasures that all the gold in Christendom could not purchase.

ALL rightly organized society is ever in a
chronic condition of civil war, where
the clashing of moral forces may be heard on
every hand. It is thus only that the good is
made to dominate the evil. Otherwise society would be a neglected garden, choked
with rank and noisome weeds, where the
flowers of beauty and harmony, and the
fruits of all ennobling virtues, would find but
a pinched and stunted growth. In this great
conflict of forces there are arrayed on one
side the promoters of all human welfare—
the friends and conservators of all that ele-
vates man in the scale of moral, spiritual and
intellectual being. On the other are the
enemies of man's truest happiness—and their
name is legion—who are ever at work seeking to drag him down nearer and nearer to
the primal types of being whence it is supposed he sprung. The tiger of the Indian
jungle is not more ferocious and merciless
than are some human tigers who fatten on

the blood of innocent souls, and who leave
mourning and desolation in their track.

In this contest for the right there is always
work and room for all. The Press, the
Church, the School, are usually, and ever
should be, the mighty Columbiads, thunder-
ing the grand lessons of life from the ram-
parts of society. And whoever gives a cup
of water to a thirsty traveler, or speaks a
kind and helping word to a fellow being in
distress, is a private soldier in the same
grand cause. And this is the conflict of the
ages—the warfare of the evermore.

All of which is preliminary to a few
thoughts, pertinent or otherwise, to a gen·
eral subject that has awakened no little in·
terest in every community, which subject
may be expressed in the form of a question,
thus : Is gambling for religious purposes
ever justifiable ? In ·no other State in the
Union are the inducements and temptations
to acquire something for nothing as great as
they are in California. Gold and silver
mining is in itself but little better than a
game of chance. It was so in the early days
of placer mining, and is more so now in the

days of quartz mining. But that bears no comparison with the wild speculative mania for stock gambling. The miner puts in his labor, and if he won the golden prize it was but the legitimate fruits of that labor. The stock gambler invests in his business no honest toil, but makes his money upon his ability to outlie somebody else. This mad passion for speculation is sapping the very foundations of society. It is wrecking the peace and happiness of multitudes.

But this is but one manifestation of the gambling spirit. It has other and darker phases—vortexes into which our young men are plunging, and where they will be engulfed forevermore.

With this peril at our doors—a vice as insidious as the malaria that feeds the plague—ought not every pulpit and press in the land to declaim against it? Who can say that our laws prohibiting gambling are unjust, or one whit too severe? Hence is it not the plain duty of every Christian man and woman, and every one who has the welfare of his fellows at heart, to strengthen the arm of the law in this behalf, and to unite in creating and sustaining a public sentiment in relation thereto, that will banish the vice from our borders, or at least drive it into the alley ways and secret corners of society, where it can no longer poison the common air we breathe.

There is no division of sentiment among thoughtful people concerning the giant vices and wrongs of the world. Murder, arson, theft, drunkenness—these overtowering sins · find naught but condemnation in every heart. But it is the smaller and more seductive vices—fashionable gambling, drinking, social dissipation, etc.,—that "stir a fever in the blood" of society, and pave the way for those greater vices, to indulge in which is moral and physical death.

The Church often preaches against the venality and licentiousness of the press ; but when the former throws the mantle of its sanctity over gambling in any form, it becomes our turn to preach the gospel of a better and purer morality.

ONLY men who are scoundrels at heart ever countenance dishonesty in others.

REAL, downright, unselfish, generous natures ought to be more numerous than they are—that is, natures who can feel an unselfish joy in the prosperity of others, even though their own lot may be a hard one,—natures that can go on foot and be glad that their neighbors are able to support a carriage and ride ; or who can rejoice that others can live in a palace, while they can afford only a humble cottage, and a rented one at that.

Some people are so constituted that they are happy only in proportion as others are miserable ;—in other words, though they may possess a reasonable measure of wealth and those external things that are supposed by many to be wholly essential to happiness, their joy would be dimmed in the presence of one who possessed a larger measure of those same externals. They must possess *more* than their neighbor, or else the mean little cross-eyed demon of envy nestles in

their bosoms and robs them of their peace of
mind.

It requires no great amount of magna-
nimity of character to be generous to those
who are beneath us in point of social position, external surroundings, or in genuine
worth of soul ; but it does really take a large
nature to be charitably and unselfishly generous towards ostentatious and purse-proud
inferiors—those whose only merit is in the
husk and not the kernel.

We can all be generous towards the dead.
Even those who in life we cared the least
for, and who were least worthy of our respect,
call forth a heart-throb of sympathy for them
in their last extremity. It is then we think
only of their virtues, and even chide ourselves for not being more generous to their
imperfections when living.

.What the world most needs is an order of
humanity that can anticipate death in the
exercise of the nobler charities—that does
not wait till the pale specter sets its seal
upon the heart of a fellow being to send forth
an impulse of sympathy in his behalf. The
world needs all its generous impulses of kind-

ness *now*, when they will do the most good.
The rich need this baptism of generosity as
well as the poor, the haughty and proud as
well as the humble.

It is every individual's right and duty to
get all out of life that properly belongs to
him ; but this he can never do if he troubles
himself much about what properly belongs
to others. He should school himself in the
philosophy that all physical or temporal be-
longings are but the veriest dross and chaff,
as compared with the precious wealth of
genuine character. That alone is enduring
—alone will stand the racket of time and the
wear of eternity.

We pity the man or woman, in the enjoyment of physical health, and with sense
enough to think they have good sense, who
can not find hights and depths of solid comfort in this life, sufficient to establish a small
paradise of their own. If they can not, they
are souls sadly out of tune with nature—a
fact which they should learn to realize, and if
possible to set themselves right before they
become permanently incapacitated for enjoying the truer life.

ILLIBERAL LIBERALISM,

"IBERALISM," so-called, is often but another name for the most intolerant bigotry. And nowhere do we find a better illustration of this fact than in the contributions to the columns of the chief organ of Liberalism in the United States—the Bos on *Investigator*. The editorials of that journal are usually not seriously open to the foregoing objection—the editor being naturally a kind-hearted man, and inclined to be considerate of the opinions of religionists— quite as much, if not more so than many religious editors are disposed to be towards him and his opinions. But some of the *Investigator's* correspondents are simply vicious in their treatment of religious questions. Serenely anchored in their own inordinate conceit, and absolutely ignorant of the vast array of psychological facts and experiences that are entirely familiar to others, and have been through all the ages, they become actually insolent in their negations of the

world of things they do not happen to know.
And this they do in the name of Liberalism.
A truly liberal man is never intolerant or
bigoted. He is modest in his doubts, and
never denies stubbornly. He studies to understand the reason of things, and to fortify
his mind with arguments—not so much to
disprove this theory or strengthen his convictions of the truth of that ; but really to
arrive, if possible, at the absolute truth. He
seeks to find out what nature means—not to
confirm what he thinks she ought to mean.

The true Liberalist will never seek to disturb the serene faith of another in religious
things, where such disturbance would tend to
seriously mar the happiness and peace of
mind of such person. There are persons the
bent of whose natures, coupled with a lifetime of pious training, are so deeply grounded
in their religious faith—so sure that theirs is
the only true way of salvation,—that to doubt,
with them, would be to so unsettle their
lives that the most serious consequences
would be apt to follow. It is not always
safe to attempt to soar on untrained wing—
to break loose from a religious anchorage

that has been the mainstay of a lifetime.   No
true Liberalist would recommend it.

There is good in all religions, and much
that is not religion.   Jew and Gentile,
Christian and pagan—all possess the common
virtues of humanity, and often its worst
vices.   Many religious people are no doubt
better men and women because of the restraining influence of their religion.   As humanity averages we should very much dislike
to reside in a community where no such
restraining influences were felt.   Law would
be powerless to protect life and property
from the viciously inclined.   If a man can
not walk uprightly and deal fairly with his
fellows, except through fear of eternal punishment, or the hope of everlasting pleasures
in another life, we would encourage him in
that belief.

We have no sympathy with that reckless
and intolerant Liberalism that would sweep
away with a breath all the safeguards of religion ; nor with that persecuting spirit that
would condemn a fellow being either because
of his belief, or non-belief.

True Liberalism is gentle and charitable,

and considerate of the opinions of others. It is the exclusive property of no class of thinkers. It is found in the church and out of it. It belongs to all broad natures and advanced souls. What the church and the world want is more of it.

SELF-DEPENDENCE.

THE greatest obstacle in the pathway of man's advancement to a higher plane of life, in all the past ages, has been his dependence upon God, rather than upon himself. He has hoped and prayed and waited for some Omnipotent, Unseen and Unknown Power to do his work for him—to pull him out of the slough of ignorance, superstition and natural cussedness—until he has become well nigh fossilized. He has watched the clashing of moral forces, all along the line of history, and has seen the world deluged in blood and tears. He has beheld nations struggle into existence and disappear in carnage and woe. And all this as though he were an idle spectator in the universe, never dreaming that this was his world, and that it was his especial business to save it from perdition.

In depending upon God to do the work of humanity we demonstrate not only our own worthlessness, but how little we understand the great and Divine plan of creation. We are not the blind, unreasoning instruments, in the hand of Omnipotence, that many, by their works at least, would have us believe. We are here for a grander purpose than it ever entered into the brain of man to imagine. We are here to act as well as to be acted upon—to work out, in and through ourselves, that truer life, that more perfect manhood, that has been the dream of the prophet and the hope of the sage, in all the unfolding ages of the world's history.

The man who prays to be led "not into temptation," should, if not strongly enough grounded in moral principle to resist temptation, keep out of temptation's way. He who prays for His "will to be done on earth as it is in Heaven," should endeavor to find out what that will is ; and, as he expects God to work through him, to begin and do a little of the work himself, and thereby show his willingness in the matter. He should stop crowding his neighbor, and should cultivate and practice the noble virtues, and set up the millennium in his own life and character. He who prays God to give him this day his daily bread, should understand that after all his praying the bread must come through his own effort. If not so then there would never be such a thing as starvation or famine, in the world. What mockery of Divine goodness it is to hear a rich man, as he gathers in his purse strings, pray to God to remember the widow and the fatherless in their affliction, to clothe the naked and feed the hungry. Why doesn't he go down into his pocket and do it himself? How can he expect God to help the poor without the use of his money?

And so in all that relates to the welfare of the race—to all social, political and moral reforms—to all mitigation of human ills—of pauperism, crime, insanity, and the disordered conditions of society and humanity of every kind—we must quit leaving this work for

God to do. If we would have it done at all
we must take the matter into our own hands.
For the only way God works in the moral
world is through human agency.

We unhesitatingly assert that the character
and quality of the human race are in the
keeping of the race, and may be made good,
bad or indifferent, as we will; that if we
should give one-half as much time and thought
to the uplifting of humanity as we do to
money-getting, it would not be fifty years
hence before we should have no use for
prisons, or insane asylums; have no tramps
nor unemployed laborers; no squalid poverty; no overcrowded cities, with their vast
multitudes of wretched and diseased humanity; no use for armies or navies, with all
their costly and barbaric appendages. How,
do you ask, could all this be accomplished ?
Simply by humanity taking the matter into
their own hands, and not waiting for Providence to do the business; or rather by
allowing Providence to commence and carry
out the work through them. There is no
good reason why society—the better portion
thereof—should not grapple with the giant

evils that beset the race, and purge the world thereof. This is by no means as difficult a task as it might seem—nothing like as difficult as it is to carry the fearful burdens we now endure.

PIETY OF FUN.

HARADES, Songs, Unique Wax Figures, Babes in the Woods, very amusing bottle performance, and other interesting amusements.' Well, I declare," remarked Spiggles to us, a few days ago, on reading the above list of attractions announced to come off at a Church Fair; " the sheep and the goats are so near alike now-a-days that it is difficult to tell where the wool ends and the hair begins." We were struck with the force of this rough-shod remark, and were led to inquire why it is that people usually imagine that in order to make one's " calling and election sure," he must necessarily wear a sombre visage, shut himself out from all the enjoyments of the world and live the life

of a gloomy ascetic! The old Calvanistic
idea that makes future happiness attainable
only through groans and tears, and that an
individual should be willing to be damned
for the glory of God, is fast fading from the
world. We believe in the religion of joy,
and the piety of innocent fun, and do not
think it is fair that the world's people should
have an exclusive patent to all the good
things in this life. Harmony is happiness ;
and the best homage that man can render to
his Creator is by living in harmony with the
laws of his own being—doing good to others
by lifting the lowly to higher planes of existence, and continually reaching outward
and upward for something higher and better.
Entertaining such opinions we can see nothing in the above bill of attractions inconsistent
with true religion, neither could we had
dancing been included. It was thus we put
the case to Spiggles, and the young man
subsided.

HE who conquers himself wins the rarest
and highest victory—a garlanded hero he
from the fiercest battle ever fought and won.

RESIGNATION,

I HAVE said—and I would not recall the words,
　　Though all of my future remain unblest,
That the pathway of thorns my feet have trod
　　Was for me of all earthly ways the best.—

That the wrecks of my hopes that have strewn the
　　shore,
　　Like stranded ships by the storm-spent sea,
Were argosies richer with precious store
　　Than all of earth's treasures were to me.

Had my life been one of indolent ease—
　　Had fortune before me her baubles spread ;
And the empty world, as I sought to please,
　　.Had it placed its emptier crown on my head,—

Had the smiles of earth and the bending skies,
　　And the pleasures of time that gladden and cloy,
Had I shared them all in their fullness of sense,
　　And nothing of earth were there left to enjoy,—

Methinks I should then have missed the prize,
　　By an infinite waste of barren years—
The gem in the soul's deep mine that lies,
　　And is wrought into shape through toil and
　　　　tears.

I ne'er should have found the hidden ore
　　Of Truth, whose marvellous golden goal
Is only reached through the drifts of life
　　By the diamond drill of a chastened soul.—

The truth, that opens the shining way
    Of trustful endurance forever more,—
And the pathway of duty is clearly lined
    Through the rifts in the clouds to the hither
      shore.

And thus have I patiently learned to bear
    The burdens and pains of life's unrest,
Thankful alike for the storm and the calm,
    And hopefully trusting that all's for the best.

GETTING religion, with some people, is a good deal like getting the measles or whooping cough. They are taught that it is something that can come to them from without only in a peculiar way, and in a certain attitude of body and mind ; when, in fact, all there is of it of any appreciable use to humanity consists simply in ceasing to do evil and learning to do well.

THE teacher who can not call forth the love of his pupils is incapable of accomplishing much success in his profession. He has mistaken his calling.

SELFISHNESS is essential to good government and the truest welfare of society.

THE fact that man possesses much of the brute element in his nature is strongly indicative of his brute origin. In tracing his ancestral line backward through the ages of his slow but certain unfoldment the thread is lost in that shadowy prophecy of the race, the huge prehistoric savage, clothed in the skins of wild beasts ; or stark beneath tropical suns ; with no implements of art or industry, no weapons of warfare save the club and stone ; a dweller in caves and hollow trees ; the companion of animals long since extinct. Bridging backwards, in imagination, a few more æons of time, and we behold him a magnificent specimen of an anthropoid ape, walking erect, shaggy and coarse, with massive chest and jaws, low frontal brain, small pointed ears, skull thick and head broad at the base, showing great tenacity of life. What a terrible but splendid beast—fierce, ferocious, wild. How he tyrannizes over his fellow-beasts—driving them from their dens without "due process of law," and taking up his own abode therein—meeting his equals in physical strength in fierce and deadly contests, and by his greater cunning, entrapping his superiors to their destruction.

The descendants of this terrible brute, in whose nature was enfolded the germs of a Shakspere, a Milton, a Rosa Bonheur and an Alice Cary, have brought down with them many of their ancestral traits. And it is to this fact we are indebted for all the inharmony and wretchedness that exist in the world. It is the wild beast in human nature that prompts the strong to oppress the weak, that withholds the needed sympathy from the poor and unfortunate—the exercise of ever blessed charity from the erring. It is the unsubdued ancestral element in man—the outcroppings of his prehistoric brute nature, when he contended with other brutes for a bone, that prompts him now to take advantage of his fellows in a bargain ; to grind one and a half per cent a month out of a poor man struggling to save his little home from the exactions of the law ; to gather to himself riches at the expense of honor ; to betray a friend ; to tyrannize over a wife ; to lead astray the young and confiding ; to steal and lie and murder ; in short to live a life that is at war with that truer life that comes only through man's unfoldment upon the higher spiritual and intellectual planes of his existence.

As the brain of man becomes finer and more spiritualized, overarching the animal and intellectual life, the meanness of his nature gradually disappears. A deep sense of justice, and a feeling of divine harmony and good will to man, take the place of that cruel selfishness that works but to mar and destroy. The man drifts farther and farther away from the crude conditions in which recorded history first found him, and comes nearer and nearer into the likeness of that ideal manhood which shall yet fill the earth in " the good time coming."

To eliminate the crude, the coarse, the animal, and take on the pure, the good, the beautiful, should be the end and aim of every individual soul. Some there are who are seeking for the best in their own lives and characters, and they are " the salt of the earth "—the leaven that shall yet permeate and reconstruct the whole.

If we only realized the help we might be to those less favored than ourselves, by the exercise of our best sympathies and charities toward them—by the encouraging and kindly spoken word—by the manifestation of a heartfelt interest in their welfare—by the radiation of that sweet influence divine which every soul has the power to impart—how rapidly would wrong, discord and unhappiness disappear from the earth. Is it not worth trying?

If the tradesman who seeks your custom under the pretext that he is selling you goods at less than cost, while at the same time he makes a reasonable profit thereon,—and the customer who takes advantage of another's necessities to pay less for an article than it is worth,—were shaken in a bag together, it would be hard to tell which would come out first.

THE use of tobacco and whisky should be regarded as justifiable grounds for divorce.

ORGANIZATION

ORGANIZATION is the secret of all success in life. It is the basis of all social order—of all national prosperity. In the church, the home, the state, it is the keystone of the arch—the chief pillar of the temple. Wherever it is not chaos reigns and the uncontrolled elements run riot through the fields of space.

Nature sets us an example of organization in all her works. We see it in the matchless mechanism of the universe,—in the harmonious movement of the planets that sweep around our sun,—in the mighty aggregation of waters that enfold our earth,—in the ebb and flow of the tides,—in the changes of the seasons,—in the mystic temple of the human soul,—in the marvellous mystery of animal life,—in the growth of a blade of grass. All is thoroughly organized, and evidently moving forward to a purpose, whose ultimate staggers conception with its possibilities.

And it is from this example man should take the hint. He will, if he is wise. He will treasure the many lessons that nature teaches him, and profit himself therein. The truest knowledge that can come to a young man or woman is that of knowing what they are here for,—for what world of use and work they were intended—for what they are best fitted to succeed in. It is a painful fact that this knowledge comes to but comparatively few. Hence the wrecks of humanity we see all around us.

Young people, in their immature ideas of life and unstable convictions of duty, are apt —to borrow a phrase from the glossary of the sportsman—to "scatter" too much. They dabble in many things, but in nothing persistently and permanently. They have not found out what they are here for, or if they have, they have not learned the art of organizing and concentrating their faculties upon the central purpose of their lives. The man without a hobby of some sort is really of but little use in the world. He must have an object in life, around which all his energies must gather, to bear him onward to success.

It is better to be a good blacksmith than a poor editor or teacher—an artist in kalsomine or whitewash, than a dauber on canvas.

Thus, in our individual natures we see the necessity for organization—the highest and truest organization—the organization that supplements and underlies all other organizations—the complete organization of the individual man. That no man is fit to govern others who has not first learned how to govern himself is a truism requiring no argument. No man is fit to lead an army, or direct any great enterprise, who has not his own faculties well in hand. Hence, whether with individual or co-operative effort, the principle is the same ; there must be a concentration of forces, working to a specific end.

I want to emphasize and impress this idea upon the minds and consciences of all young people. In the best light of your own intelligence and judgment, settle down upon some fixed line of action—upon some life work—and then bend all your faculties, all the forces of your natures, in that direction. Do not conclude hastily, but when your conclusions are once formed, do not swerve from the end in view by so much as a hair's breadth. Resolve upon success. No matter what obstacles stand in the way, go at them with a resolute will, and surmount them, or die trying.

This is the secret of success in life, in any and every department of human action.

Promiscuous novel reading, the frivolities of fashion, and of that addle-brained humbug called society, the many enticements to idleness and uselessness, all combine to unsettle the minds of young persons, and unfit them for that rigorous application necessary to enable them to climb the shining hights of success.

O, yes, it is nice to dance and play, and have a jolly time—nice to fritter away the golden hours of life's sunny morning, like a butterfly basking in the glamour of the new born day ; but ah, there comes a time when you must needs grapple with the stern realities of existence, when the battle of life will open out before you, and when you will need large resources of character to tide you over life's rough places.

PASSING ON.

.

"Leaves have their time to fall,
And flowers to wither at the north wind's breath,
And stars to set, but all—
Thou hast all seasons for thine own, O, Death."

THERE is no religion however true, or sincerely believed in ; no philosophy however consoling, that can fully reconcile us to death. To those of us with whom faith is supplemented by the absolute knowledge of the spirit's existence beyond the confines of this mortal life, and who, if any, are possessed of a philosophy that should soothe, and comfort, and sustain us in the trying hour when our loved ones pass over the dark river—to us, even, death has a nameless dread. Our hearts rebel against it, and we ofttimes refuse to be comforted. Especially is this true when death lays its chilling hand upon the young—upon the children of our love.

The gray-haired sire, who has lived his allotted years, and fulfilled his mission on earth, may sink to sleep in Nature's enfolding arms as calmly and sweetly as the tired babe is lulled to rest upon its mother's breast. We are prepared, in a measure, for death when it comes in the fullness of time to the aged. Reason then teaches us to accept it as a wise fulfillment of law. And if such an one has lived wisely, made good use of himself, and left the world better than he found it, we know that death to him is a glorious translation to a higher life ; that with his treasured wealth of character he will be fully prepared for the fellowship of those shining ones that live just beyond the veil.

But when death comes to the child, or to the young man just entering upon the busy scenes of life, it has a much sadder aspect. And yet there is a consolation in this thought : Nature aims to complete whatever she undertakes. The human spirit once individualized and started on its long journey, will be taken care of, never fear. If it fail of obtaining its proper measure of earthly experience, we doubt not ways and means will be provided for its securing what will be equivalent to such experiences elsewhere. Nature is ample in her resources. She is a gentle and impartial mother, and, in time or eternity, will, we believe, give her children all a fair start on the road to happiness. The journey may be longer for some than for others, but it will lead to the same blissful home in the vast and eternal Beyond. Some may tread the thorny path of sorrow with bleeding feet—be hampered and surrounded by physical conditions that impede the spirit's growth—but our loving Mother understands all that. She knows that we are not always responsible for what we are—that our natures at best are but inherited—have come down to us through an ancestry that reaches away back into infinity. She realizes the temptations and trials through which we must needs pass—the physical infirmities and diseases to which we are subject. She has an infinity of ways, an infinity of room and an infinity of time in which to perform her work. And we doubt not she will do it well.

Then may we not hope that death is but the passing on to another stage of existence ; that the spirit, unable to cope with its earthly conditions, breaks its mortal bonds and is borne away to the companionship of loved ones gone before ; that there the child will find gentle protection and tender care ; the misguided and erring, wise counselors and true and loving friends? Removed from the besetting temptations and surroundings of earth, may it not be that the real work of growth will begin, and be carried forward, by a law of eternal progress, to a full and happy fruition ?

Could we inquire of our loved ones passed to the hither shore, " How is it with thee ?" and could we hear the answer they would send back to us from their spirit home, we doubt not that answer would be, " All is well." They would tell us that they rejoiced that their earth life was over, and their sorrows and sufferings at an end. They would send back words of greeting to the loved ones left behind. They would urge us to be patient and trusting to the end, discharging every known duty to ourselves and to our fellow beings. They would assure us that when at last our earthly pilgrimage should be o'er, they would be there to give us a joyous welcome to their home in the beautiful Sum mer Land.

DON'T be selfish, or mean, or narrow-minded—if you can help it. Don't consider it your duty to be a common carrier for any sort of scandal. Don't trifle with those you love, nor tread on the heart of a friend. Don't meddle with other people's business. Don't think evil of any one, even of those you do not like. The world is wide enough for all—leave them alone. Don't try to pull down those above you ; but always seek to lift those beneath you up to your level. Don't make yourself disagreeable to any one, simply because you know how. Don't yield servile submission to tobacco, whisky, or any other debasing habit ; but have manhood and womanhood enough to be decent and wholesome, and masters of your own bodies. Don't be contented with emptiness of heart or brain ; but cultivate the gentle amenities of life, and store your mind with useful knowledge. Don't be suspicious of others who are just as good as you are, and perhaps a little better, Don't be a fool.

WHAT OF THE NIGHT?

WATCHMAN, what of the night? Do the heavens indicate fair weather or foul, for the coming day? In short, what are the signs of the times?

There has never been a period in the world's history when such general and widespread unrest prevailed in the minds of men as at the present time. The deep sea of human thought seems lashed into mountain waves that break and foam along the rocky shores of time, undermining and overturning many a consecrated monument of tradition that but recently seemed as impregnable as the everlasting hills. With the modern liberty and license of thought no subject is too sacred for investigation; and many of the profoundest thinkers of the world are to-day found peering into the most sacred places— into venerated crypts and sanctuaries, where never before profane eye has dared to penetrate. Religion is undergoing a change as marvelous as the birth of a world. Science

is divesting it of its crudities and inconsisten-
cies, and reason is adding to and adorning it
with more and more rational interpretations.

In the civil and political world, likewise,
we find agitation and commotion everywhere
manifest. As thought begins to permeate
the mass of mind, convulsion and revolution
follow ; and old and long tried forms of
government are being subjected to ordeals as
crucial as the judgment of the ages. Our
own republican institutions were never subjected to so severe a strain ; and, in fact, to
the minds of many of our political econo-
mists, the question of the ability of a mixed
and heterogeneous people to govern themselves is by no means clear. Well may they
ask, If the ignorant and down-trodden masses
of the Old World are incapable of self-government, in their own countries, as they
doubtless are, wherein does that incapacity
cease upon their translation to our shores?

Here, too, after a century of growth and
prosperity, we find ourselves confronted by
new and undreamed of obstacles in the shape
of an unemployed, useless and unnecessary
humanity—of muscle supplemented by ma-

chinery—of strange phases of oppression—all complicated factors in the problem of self-government, the solution of which is yet involved in much uncertainty.

And then in the social world we find a very maelstrom of agitation, with threatening thunder-bolts all around the sky. Inharmony in marital life is peopling the world with discordant and murderous elements, fatal to the truest welfare of society. Divorces, which in past ages were almost unknown, have come to number nearly one-third the marriages. Our prisons and insane asylums are overflowing with diseased and disordered humanity as the fruits of this inharmony; while our great cities swarm with multitudes of badly organized, wretched and half-starved beings whose presence in the world is a calamity and a curse, and who never should have been suffered to exist.

What means all this commotion? Is the world growing worse, and is our civilization a failure? Perhaps the latter, in a measure, but surely not the former. Never was the world so blessed with grand, enlightened men and women as now—never such an array of

noble thinkers, philosophers or scholars.
While each former age has produced its few,
this has produced its multitude. Out of
the clashing and chaos of human affairs are
evolving nobler types of manhood and
womanhood than, with rare exceptions, any
that history records. For amid all the inharmony of the world there are divine harmonies radiating and orbing all, along the
lines of which some souls are mounting to
sublimer hights of goodness and power ; and
thus is each age a step in advance of the pre-
ceding one, and in each we behold the prophecy of a better age to come.

THE whisperer of scandal, or the carrier of
gossip, leaves a slimier track than a poisoned
reptile—pollutes the fair, beautiful world
around with a blast deadlier than the "red-
hot lipped simoon."

IT is the duty of Society, as far as possible,
to remove all temptation to a dissolute life
from the reach of those who lack the moral
firmness to resist its vitiating and seductive
influence.

ACROSS THE BAR.

Inscribed to the Memory of Capt. Francis Connor, late of
the steamship Oregon, plying between San Fran-
cisco and Portland, Oregon.

A SHIP sailed out to an unknown sea,
    Bound for a shadowy port afar ;
Out where the waves of death run high,
    It sinks from our sight across the bar ;—
Across where the hidden breakers lie,
    And the dangerous reefs of time enfold
Full many a ship with its treasures rare,
    And many a noble seaman bold.

It bears away from our saddened gaze,
    And the hearts and home of his earthly love,
The form of a sailor true and brave,
    From the shores of earth to the realm above.
His barque is freighted with noble deeds,
    And generous thoughts for all mankind,
And from his soul o'er the water speeds
    A prayer for the loved ones left behind.

And here by the wave-washed shore we stand
    Where the tides eternally ebb and flow,
Watching our ships go out to sea,
    Bearing our fondest hopes below.
But by faith we see the beckoning hand
    Of angels reaching across the bar,
To welcome our loved ones over the strand,
    To the shining way with its " gate ajar."

Note. The Bar at the mouth of the Columbia River is regarded
as the most dangerous of any upon the Pacific Coast. Capt.
Connor was noted for his skill in making the passage.

"ACT WELL YOUR PART."

OUR happiness in this life depends not so much on circumstances or surroundings, as in our determined efforts to do our best in all conditions in which we are placed. Our common heritage is more or less allied to sorrow and pain, but we have within ourselves the antidote of heart-sunshine that will alleviate, if not remove many of our troubles. But we persistently reject the means of happiness that lie within our reach, by ignoring present small pleasures, in hopes of enjoying greater ones in the future good time coming, which always keeps just ahead, and is therefore unattainable. We cultivate little cares till they sometimes attain enormous growth, by constantly dwelling on them and dolefully rehearsing them to our friends, when we should do our best to try to rise above them. In the most difficult and trying conditions there will often be a bright side, which, if seized upon, will lead one straight out of tangled paths into the light ;

and it is well to bear this continually in mind,
" Act well your part, there all the honor lies."

WHAT WE DIFFER ABOUT.

THERE are really but few points of
difference between honest men in matters essential to human happiness, here or
hereafter. They all mean right, no matter of
what creed or of no creed—Christian, Jew,
pagan, or heathen ; infidel or atheist. It is
usually, in fact we may say always, of those
things which men know the least, and of
which little or nothing can ever be known,
that they differ and wrangle about the most
and loudest. They can readily agree in their
opinions upon what they really know, or
upon principles of right and justice. Whoever asserts that it is wrong to steal, or bear
false witness, will find no opponents among
honest men. Definitions of right and wrong
really vary but little with enlightened minds ;
and there will be found to be a hundred

points of agreement between them to one of disagreement.

It is about the essential things of life, concerning which men can best agree, that make society pleasant and promotive of the truest happiness to its individual members. This common level of social life should be clearly defined in every mind, leaving the individual at liberty to traverse the byways and jungles of thought unmolested. In other words, we should learn to agree in those matters which best conserve the common good, and be willing to disagree in all things else. Common courtesy should teach us to be considerate and respectful of the opinions of others, however they may differ from our own. Dogmatism is always something to be deprecated as unworthy a noble mind. It is really indicative of ignorance. It is never so pronounced as with small and uncultured minds. For one to assert positively that he is right and his neighbor wrong, concerning what neither of them knows anything about, is as absurd as for two blind men to fall out concerning the nature of light. And yet there have been more bruised hearts and broken heads growing out of just such dogmatic assertion than the world has any idea of.

But we rejoice that the world is growing wiser in this respect. Good men and women of any sect, or of no sect, look so much alike in dress and general appearance, now-a-days, and are so much alike in manner and purpose, that no one can distinguish the difference, even if any such difference existed. Men no longer wear their faith upon their sleeves—in the cut of their coats or color of their neckties—but in their hearts and lives. We judge of them by other standards of value than by their professions of creeds, or the length of their faces on Sunday. No amount of piety, that is not well flanked and supported by good deeds, will any longer save a man in the eyes of the church or the world. Enlightened thought everywhere has come to regard goodness as very much of one quality, no matter by whom practiced. This is as it should be. It shows that the world is unfolding in the right direction. It is a prophecy of the coming time when the common plane of thought will be so broad that there will be but little room for side issues, and when such differences of opinion as we may have will be so insignificant comparatively as scarcely to create a ripple on the deep sea of thought.

The world will become wiser and better just as fast as we are willing that it should,— whenever we are ready to " pool our issues " and unite in a common purpose for the common good.

VALUE OF RICHES.

"WHAT is he worth ? " is a question often asked with reference to the financial standing of some man before the world—as though the all in all of value embraced in the word " what " consisted of houses and lands, of a huge rent-roll, a vast accumulation of Government bonds and a plethoric bank account. There are, however, other and infinitely higher standards of value for determining the real genuine worth of a man, which are seldom taken into the account—

standards as much above those of a money
consideration as the star-gemmed sky is above
the desert of Sahara.

What is he worth? "Well, they say he
is worth a million—two millions—five millions."   Is that all?   "All?   What would
you have more?" Everything more. His
millions are but the veriest dross and rags,
without some golden stores of manhood behind them—some sparkling diamonds of
sterling character—to back them up with,
and utilize them for his own highest good,
and the welfare of his fellows.

Take your average millionaire—your
Stewarts, Vanderbilts, Astors,—how did they
acquire their vast possessions of earthly
treasure? By the exercise of a greedy acquisitiveness that was deaf to every voice of
humanity ; by the rise in property values
caused by the labor of others ; by the thumb-
screws of usury on the humble homes and
holdings of the poor ; by purchased favorit-
ism in legislation and law ; by oppression,
extortion and tyranny ; in short, by the
crushing out in their own souls of every noble
and generous impulse, and the development

of a selfishness as hard and cruel as "the pestilence that walketh in darkness," or the hungry wolf of famine that gnaws at the vitals of the poor. What are such men worth? They are worth the lime in their bones, the iron in their blood, the carbon and oxygen in their fat and muscles—they are worth the elements which they received from generous Nature to piece out their physical organisms. And when Nature receives back her own, as she is sure to in the end, she doubtless feels, if she reasons, as did the poor parson whose hat was circulated among a parsimonious audience for contributions, but which was returned empty—he thanked the Lord that his hat had been returned to him. So will Nature thank God that she has received back her raw material for a man, and will seek to make a better investment the next time.

Except in cases of inherited or accidental wealth, we hold that it is only by the exercise of the baser faculties of the mind that large possessions can be acquired. If acquired in the ordinary business pursuits of life, it must necessarily be by taking undue advantage of others. For no man, by his own hands, or a fair use of the labor of other hands, can honestly amass much more than a fair competency ; or than, if reasonably liberal and mindful of the interests of others, will secure for him a comfortable old age. This proposition is self-evident.

He who adds nothing to the sum total of human happiness ; who bears no burden cheerfully ; who aggregates to himself riches and power but to oppress ; who assuages no sorrow and wipes away no tear ; but lives the life of the horse leech and sponge, blesses the world only in his "taking off." Of his earthly substance we may erect costly monuments to his memory ; but what a stupendous sarcasm ! Who would not rather live in the cherished thoughts of a grateful posterity, enshrined in the souls of those he had lived to bless and ennoble, than wear another Cheops above his useless dust ?

No, a thousand times no ; riches do not constitute the all of worth. The brave, true soul, that patiently and faithfully fills his allotted place in life, shedding upon all around the aroma of generous deeds ; with ever a helping hand and an encouraging word for a struggling brother—though he may be empty of purse and scrip, and "have not where to lay his head," is, nevertheless, the possessor of treasures that a Crœsus might envy. For such a soul there is no death. It shines out brighter and brighter with the ages.

CALLOUSED SYMPATHIES.

THE present anamalous condition of society, with its constant and extra demands upon the charitable for the relief of the laborless and destitute, is no doubt working a baneful influence upon the hearts and consciences of the benevolent, in drying up the fountains of their charities, and making them as hard and heartless as the skinflints of society, whose hearts were never warmed with a generous impulse. They are overburdened with the sorrows and necessities of others, until they are inclined to rebel in spirit against the whole business, and as a

matter of self-protection close their hearts
and their purses to the piteous pleadings of the
poor. Thus are they becoming calloused to
those tender sympathies and gentle humanities which lift man above the hard, cold level
of unfeeling and unsympathetic selfishness.

This condition of things is greatly to be
deplored ; for whatever may happen to the
race, it can not afford to lose any of its good
qualities. It has none to spare. On the
other hand it ought to be making a sure and
steady advance on the road to righteousness,
by cultivating every virtue and laying in a
good stock of character for the time to come.
We do not think a man can well have too
much of humanity about him—too much
of charity for the misfortunes and wretchedness of his fellow beings. At the same time
he owes a duty to himself, and in the be-
stowal of his charities he should do so within
the bounds of reason, and not allow the
exercise of his generous impulses to wreck
his own health or happiness. (This advice
will strike most people as wholly unnecessary!

We believe that every individual has the
right to all the happiness he can find, pro-

vided, in obtaining the same, he appropriates
what properly belongs to nobody else. It is
his duty to make the most of this life, and
get all the good out of it that is rationally
possible. He can not do this if he allows
his spiritual or intellectual unfoldment to be
retarded from any cause.

Nature wisely conceals from us, except in
a meagre way, the sufferings she inflicts upon
others. She knows that most of us have all
the troubles and heart-aches of our own that
we ought to endure, or can well bear up
under. And yet there is no soul so completely bankrupt, both in worldly wealth and
in the finer humanities, as to have nothing to
spare for others—nothing of needed temporal
assistance, or of sympathy or brotherly love.
If such there be they are to be pitied. For
them there is no blessing in the beautiful
sunshine, nor in the melody of the birds or
rippling brooks. The glory of the earth and
the grandeur of the heavens have no voice
for their ears. They are souls out of tune,
and can only give forth jangling and discordant sounds.

It should be the aim and ambition of all to

get themselves in tune—in harmony with the universe,—to find out as nearly as possible, what Nature means with them, and then lend a helping hand to the turning out of a good job. Nature furnishes the raw material of manhood, and she expects us to work it into shape. The material may not all be of first-class quality ; in fact some of it may be badly damaged by ancestral taint ; yet the true theory is to make the best use of such material as we may chance to have. It is no doubt more creditable to some people that they are only average sinners, than for others that they are shining saints. In the former case it is a wonder they are no worse, considering the circumstances of their birth and early training. In the latter, it is a wonder, for the same reason, how they could have been anything else.

All that the good Father requires of any man is to do the best he can.

As between a good heart and a sound head, we would prefer the former—in a next-door neighbor !

I T is impossible that all men should see all things in the same light, owing to variations in capacity for observation, in development of brain, in natural bent and educational drift of thought, and from various other causes which are patent to every student of human nature. It is doubtless well for us that there is this diversity among men, else this would be a very tame world. If all were true Christians there would be no work of reformation for Christians to perform. If there were no temptations to sin there would be no particular virtue in goodness, on the same principle that if there was no alcohol in the world there would be no name for temperance—no virtue in abstinence.

It is impossible for the mind to reason itself into the belief that white is black, or that the sun rises in the west. There are propositions outside the realm of natural facts, propositions widely divergent in their character, which some minds can never accept as positive truths. Thus it seems that we are here in accordance with a great plan of the Universe—here to struggle with conditions and circumstances that seem essential to our growth and development as rational beings, and without which we should be mere passive instruments in the hands of Nature, as characterless and helpless as the log that floats upon the current of the river, outward and onward to some unknown sea.

We look around us and we see doubters on every side—honest and thoughtful doubters—doubters thronging the avenues of trade—scientific doubters—good men and noble women, who aim to walk uprightly in the world ; who pay their honest debts ; who wrong no man, and whose hearts are filled with good will towards all the race. We shall not argue with those good people who believe these, their doubting fellow mortals, are all on the broad road to ruin. We simply know that they exist in vast numbers, and that they are seemingly beyond the reach of conviction of the errors of their opinions, if errors they are. And yet are they wholly without religious feeling?

Surely not, if the exercise of charity, brotherly love, and all those virtues which adorn human character count for aught.

Again, we look around us and we behold misery, crime and ignorance everywhere—fellow-beings groveling in grossness, and dead to every impulse of a noble manhood. We see on every hand the result of violated law—children robbed of their natural birthright to healthful bodies—the world peopled with moral deformities—the strong oppressing the weak—night prevailing over right. Here is a field for believers and unbelievers alike—a common ground of religious usefulness that should know neither sect nor sex. It is the broad field of humanity, where all true men and women can meet and work to a common purpose. And how vast the work, how great the need of clear conceptions of human duty, and of an enlightened understanding that makes its pathway plain.

When mankind stops wasting its substance of brain power and physical effort upon abstractions, and lays its hand firmly to the plow-share of practical reform, we shall have less use for prisons, for asylums for the indigent and insane—less poverty and in-harmony in the world, and a higher average standard of human happiness. And when it learns more fully that true happiness comes only with right living and right doing, we shall cease to cavil at the opinions or beliefs of others. It is what a man does for human-ity—not what dogmas he believes in—that will then express the mint value of the man. Would that we all had more charity for what may seem to us errors of opinions in others.

HE would be considered insane who should, without chart or compass, sail out upon the ocean, and, with no port in view, drift hither and thither upon the vast deep ; and yet multitudes of souls float out upon the mysti-cal sea of life as aimless and objectless—no star or beacon light to guide them o'er the dreary waste.

IT is better to live rich—that is, rich in the sumptuous enjoyment of all soulful things— and die poor in purse, than to live an empty soul-life, and leave millions for heirs to quarrel over.

SINGLE BLESSEDNESS.

Resolved,—That an unmarried man is happier, and can do more good, than a married man.

THE above resolution constituted the theme of discussion by a literary society of Oakland, recently. As regards the " happiness " part of the proposition ; there is a wide diversity of opinion as to what constitutes happiness. If sleeping alone in a hog pen, with no one to scratch your back, and with freedom to chew tobacco in bed and expectorate where you please ;—if feeding on boarding-house hash,) a compound of stale beef, cockroaches and red hair) and having a joint ownership with the chambermaid in the use of your tooth-brush ;—if living selfishly for your own enjoyment, with the feeling gradually creeping over you that you are of no earthly use in the world ; if, when you die, to be unfeelingly chucked into a hole in the ground, without one tear of fond remembrance to moisten the earth that rattles down upon your coffin ;—if this condition of things constitutes happiness, then most assuredly is a single life especially conducive of happiness. Still, one had better endure all this, and infinitely more of the same sort, than to be yoked for life to a good-for-nothing woman—too many of whom modern society fashions and turns out upon the world. But a good, true, noble loving woman, there is nothing like her.

HE who would attain the truest happiness must forget self, and seek to lift the burdens from weary laden souls,—scattering the flowers of kindness and sympathy, and making light the hearts of those around. Then comes the joy and consciousness of having done some good to others, which brings the sweetest balm to our own hearts. And he who does most good to his fellow-man knows a bliss that the narrow, selfish man can never feel.

THE rapid march of invention, during the last quarter of a century, has so revolutionized our systems of labor as to make the readjustment of man to the soil and to the sources of subsistence a necessity.

IT is safe to assume that all humanity desire happiness, and any failure to attain the fruition of this desire, must be from lack either of proper conditions for right enjoyment, or of proper effort to that end. The want of proper conditions—such as inherited tendencies to disease, strong natural bias to evil, and unfavorable surroundings in early life—are all beyond the control of the individual; hence the manhood or womanhood of every person must necessarily take its complexion largely from circumstances beyond and outside of their own volition. This should teach us charity towards others worse conditioned than ourselves; while at the same time it should stimulate us to put forth every effort in our power to master the results of bad conditions in our own natures. It should also teach us the importance of so living that we may not transmit to others the evils that have been handed down to us.

"Cease to do evil and learn to do well."

This is the lesson from which is evolved all reform in individual or public life. When a man learns that the right thing is the best thing—whether the lesson comes to him by a gradual unfoldment of the understanding, through the exercise of enlightened reason, or by some sudden evolution of feeling radiating his nature to a nobler purpose—he is on the right track.

What we want in practical, every-day life, is an article of humanity that will "wash"— a fabric of character that will "wear," and if possible improve with age. We want less crowding—less selfishness among men. We want more of that outflowing brotherhood that can sympathize with another's woe, and that is ready to reach out a friendly hand to help pull another's load. We want well balanced heads and warm, humane hearts— not frisking in senseless antics on Pisgah's hights to-day, and to-morrow groping and wailing by the "cold streams of Babylon," but with unfaltering steadiness and firmness —with an uprightness and integrity of character that knows no deviation—moving right onward to a purpose—the highest purpose—a grand and noble manhood and womanhood.

Here is a common plane of thought and action upon which all true men can meet and labor. It is our everlasting quibbling about methods that destroys one-half the good that people would do in the world. We are not content to let others think as they will, even though the outcome of their thought, coupled with their aim in life, means all one thing, at least so far as the general welfare and happiness of mankind in this life is concerned. We live in the eternal, ever present Now. If we make the best use of our lives in the present tense, it is the best that we can do.

MANY people waste the best portion of their lives in worrying about what others may think and say of them ; when if they would "let the world wag," and endeavor to live out, in their own lives, their best ideals of manhood, or womanhood, they would find themselves enjoying a far greater measure of happiness.

NIGHT.

THE sun upon his purple pillow rests
Behind the western hills.   An azure cloud,
  Fringed with the glory of departing day,
  As gorgeous as e'er Israel's legions led,
  Stands sentinel above his royal couch.
One by one the golden buds of night
Unfold their stary petals to my gaze,—
The constellated armies of the skies, ·
A voiceless host, are ever marching on,
With silent tread and majesty supreme,
In the high path of heaven's unbounded space.

        The winds are lulled to sleep ;
No sound of rustling leaf, nor insect hum,
Nor din of busy life, breaks on my ear ;
And yet a melody pervades all space,
As of unnumbered harps by angels played,—
Angelic choirs, whose silken fingers sweep
The silv'ry chords, until the vast expanse
Seems filled with the soft symphony of Heaven.
Alone I stand upon the silent heath,—
A worthless speck upon the object glass
Of God's great microscope.   Unnumbered worlds,
Whose vastness staggers thought, around me blaze,
Filling immensity with beams of light.

For what was all this wondrous glory made ?
I send the dove of thought from this frail ark,
That coasts along the shores of time, away
To yon bright spheres ; I charge it penetrate
The mystery profound, and bring me back
Some branch of knowledge from those upper worlds.
A bootless errand. Wearied with its flight,
Back to my longing soul it comes again,
Bringing no token—leaving all in gloom.

Mark yon lurid gleam ;
As though a star from its fixed center shot,
Trailing a fiery shaft athwart the sky,
Then fading softly into silent naught,
Leaving the dark more dense. A moment here
It flashed across my wond'ring soul ; the next,
Went out in night forever.

But lo ! what splendor breaks upon my sight,
Paling the stars along the northern sky !
Now jetting up in streams of rosy light,
Until the firmament of heaven glows
And flashes with supernatural fire !
Now from the zenith drooping gently down,
Until the earth with glory is festooned,
And curtained in with soft auroral light.

Such are the glorious visions of the night,
Lifting the soul to higher realms of thought,
In contemplating the infinity of God.

WHAT IS RELIGION?

WHAT is religion? Perhaps no better answer can be given to the question than this : that it is the practice of goodness. Whether this answer embodies the all of religion, or not, as doubtless many will say not, certain it is that a religion without the practice of goodness is no better, if not worse (and generally worse), than no religion at all. It is the shell without the kernel—the casket without the jewel—the shadow without the substance. To the practice of this kind of religion—a religion with the element of goodness left out— nay be attributed all the cruelties and crimes of martyrdom, and all the fierce persecution for opinion's sake, that have disgraced and blackened the ages, and left their ineffaceable stain upon the church. Although in the sunburst of enlightened thought of these "latter days," the terrible physical evils that followed the practice of a goodless, or God-less, religion in former times, are impossible forever more ; nevertheless the world, or

rather the church, is largely overstocked
with a modified form of the same article.

Goodness, to be thoroughly genuine,—
that is to possess staying qualities,—must be
" bred in the bone." A fair article may be
acquired, perhaps, by what is called con-
version—a sudden or spasmodic revolution
of the moral nature, like a change of the
polarity of the earth, or something of that
sort,—but it is too apt to be only superficial
in its character—hardly skin deep. It seldom
gets down through the froth of the emotions
and strikes its grappling irons into the firm
and solid substance of the soul. It is an
impulsive sort of goodness, that operates
only in the heat of a revival, and then con-
geals into a chronic condition of irreligious
selfishness, if not of positive badness.

The Great Spirit of Life, Law and Love
works upon the moral forces of the world
only through human agencies. Each individual soul is a self-constituted and divinely
appointed and commissioned Committee of
the Whole to carry out that work. The
man who prays God to bless the widow and
the fatherless, to clothe the naked and feed

the hungry ; or to do any other act or thing
that he has it in his power to perform himself, is simply wasting his breath and trifling
with his own moral nature. God doesn't
work in that way. And yet how much of
this sort of praying is done. It is the
practice of religion with the soul of religion
left out.

If the money and time we spend in that
kind of religious worship that endeavors, by
penitence and tears, to placate a wrathful
and revengeful God ; or, by high-sounding
praise and hallelujahs, to tickle the ears of a
vain one, were devoted to the simple practice
of goodness, isn't it barely possible that this
would be a better and happier world, and
that the Being we seek to honor would think
all the better of us for it? At any rate,
would we not learn thereby to think better
of ourselves?

The religion that troubles itself about the
heathen in pagan lands, or worries itself sick
over the sins of an unregenerate world,
while at the same time its neighbor across
the way is struggling with the " wolf at the
door," or perishing for a sympathetic word,

isn't worth harvesting. It wouldn't yield a bushel to the acre ; and mostly cheat at that.

If this world is ever to be made better,— and that it will be is a moral certainty, for eternal progress is a law of nature,—it must be accomplished through human agency. No matter what power may be behind man and working through him, he must perform the work himself. No one will do it for him. He must answer his own prayers. And a first rate place to begin this work is right in his own soul.

Most people are reasonably good when they find out what ails them. All they want is to have their faces set in the right direction, when they will walk right. With our noble co-laborers in the church and the world, be it ours to assist in setting them right.

HE who thinks for himself, and sometimes thinks wrongly, possesses an individuality and self-reliance that constitute sterling elements of character that many a saint, schooled in other modes of thought, has been lacking in.

TRUTH SPOKEN IN JEST.

WHAT'S yours is mine, and what's mine is my own." There is many a truth spoken in jest, and perhaps there is none more truthful, or more often spoken by married men than that we have chosen above for a few words for comment.

A man and woman enter into joint partnership for life. Say, each brings to the partnership some little means—just sufficient to obtain a humble start in the world. Perhaps they buy land, and by hard work, in time, obtain a competency. All of this time the husband handles all the company funds, and generally doles out to the wife, grudgingly and complainingly, such pittances as she may absolutely need for her personal use. As a rule, she works more hours, and performs more hard manual labor, in proportion to her strength, than does her husband. This is evident from the fact that he grows strong and robust, while she shows the signs of toil and care, and is often broken down in

health from overwork and child-bearing before she reaches middle age. Not a dollar
of all their joint earnings can she call her
own. If she wants a little money never so
much, she must explain to him all the whys
and wherefores, and render a strict account
for every cent expended.

What is the result of all this unfairness?
We could cite numerous instances where
wives and daughters have had to resort to a
system of petty larceny to obtain what was
justly their due—actually picking the pockets
of the husband and father at convenient
opportunities, and following up the practice
for years. Who can blame them? and yet
what sort of effect must such practices
naturally have upon the children of such
parents? Cases are not rare where the
mother, driven through the parsimony of
the husband to steal in this manner, has
branded the bias and purpose of theft upon
the soul of her unborn offspring.

But some one may ask, Isn't the husband
the natural head of the family, and hence the
proper judge of their needs? We answer,
that the wife is entitled by right to her

proper share of the company earnings, and
to be treated as an equal in the family. If
she chooses to leave her share in his hands
for investment, as most wives would, that is
her privilege. What we insist upon is that
she shall have such portion of the joint earn
ings as she may need, without question.
Industrious wives are generally safe bankers.
They will economize and save in a hundred
ways that a man would never think of.
They never spend their money in saloons,
nor for cigars, nor do they bet on horse
races. They can certainly be trusted with
their own.

We will venture to suggest what we regard
as the true policy in family finances : First,
the wife should have a weekly or monthly
allowance, proportioned to the value of her
services as housekeeper and the amount of
the husband's income. The children, also,
as soon as they arrive at a suitable age,
should have their separate allowances, from
which they should be expected to clothe
themselves and defray all of their personal
expenses. This would teach them business
principles. They would soon learn to econ-

omize—to live within their means, and get something ahead. The fact of possession carries with it a sense of responsibility and dignity. By this arrangement the home would be exalted, and the family relation made more harmonious and attractive. It is humiliating to a sensitive woman to be always obliged to crave as a favor what she feels in her soul is hers of right.

Consider these things, O, ye skinflint husbands!

The man who imagines the world owes him a living mistakes his own importance in the economy of the universe. The world owes him nothing. On the other hand, he is indebted to the world for the gases and minerals of his worthless body, which he ought to settle for, and the sooner the better.

There is no credit in sobriety to one who dislikes the taste of liquor, nor in purity of life to one who has never been tempted.

The profoundest vacuum in the world is the vacuum of an empty soul.

WORK.

THE Scriptural injunctions to "take no thought of the morrow," and to "sell *all* that thou hast and give to the poor," were probably never intended to be lived up to strictly ; but rather that one should not set his whole heart on worldiy gain, and should give as liberally as his means will admit to relieve the suffering and misery which everywhere abound in the land. Work is an absolute necessity for a healthy condition of body and mind ; and whoever works with a purpose *must* take "thought of the morrow," and extend his plans into the future. Idleness is the mother of vice. Constant physical labor is the only reliable protector of virtue. There is nothing that subdues the passions and keeps the blood tame like hard work. It is a hundred fold more effective than prayer, as the experience of the Church and the world abundantly proves. Not that we would underrate prayer, which in its true meaning is an aspiration—a desire—for something better. Life should be a constant prayer. But prayer is not of the least account without works. The Lord helps those only who help themselves. All nature is governed by fixed and unalterable laws. Whoever lives in harmony with these laws will be happy. Blessings flow in fixed channels. To enjoy the blessings we must go where they are—they will never come to us. Work, if you would reap the richest rewards of life. Work, if you would live in the sunshine, and enjoy the fruits of contentment. Work on and work ever, hoping, trusting, and growing into the full development of an upright, noble and glorious manhood.

THE thief who steals my cloak has no right to my coat, and it is not sound morality to give it to him.

THE world is wide enough for people to disagree in without the necessity for breaking each other's head.

IN starting out in political life every young man should be quite sure he is right before he goes ahead.

A SPRING MORNING,

THE joy of a Spring morning melts over a waking world. The air is cool and soft with exhaling moisture, and balmy with the breath of many flowers. The sunshine that tides over the eastern hills and pours its effulgent waves of glory down upon the plain below, breaks into golden ripples among the verdure of forest and field. From a thousand bird throats, from the lips of the opening rose, from the diamond eyes of the dew-drop, from the great heart of Nature throbbing with life and love, bursts forth an anthem of gladness to the new born day. How calm and beautiful is our Mother Earth—so old, and yet so fresh and fair.

Upon such a morning as this, with the soul in tune with Nature's diviner harmonies, one can hardly realize that discord and in-harmony exist in the world—that hate finds a lodgment in human breasts—that man could ever be at war with man. All Nature is full of beckoning hands and welcoming voices, inviting man to a truer and higher life. She says to him from the heart of the rose, Be beautiful in soul as I am, and fragrant with the aroma of good deeds. She calls to him from mountain hights of eternal snows, saying, Be white and pure as I am, and warm in heart as the fires that glow down deep in my own bosom. She speaks to him from the towering oak, hoary with the breath of centuries, Be strong and firm as I am, and deeply rooted in manly principles, that shall withstand the shocks of time and the blasts of adversity. In gentle rain and warm sunshine, that bless alike the growing corn and the useless weed, she says to him, Give as I give ; be broad in your charities ; be liberal and grand. She calls to him from rippling stream, from deeply-flowing river, from broad and restless ocean ;—she urges him by hints, prophecies and warnings ;—she appeals to him through the laughter of children, the blush on the cheek of innocent girlhood, the cooing of the turtle dove to its mate ; she pleads with him in the heart-throes of anguish, in the decrepitude of old age, in the faint whispers of the dying ;—she

invites him by every impulse of her own
great heart—by every noble aspiration of his
own soul—to come up higher—to live a
nobler and truer life.

And yet how few there are who heed
Nature's admonitions or profit by her lessons.
With thoughts and eyes bent earthwards,
they never see the stars that shine forever
in the "blue vault of night" above them.
They grovel among the slums of earth-life,
in a realm of unworthy thoughts and desires,
raking up garbage instead of golden grain.
They think meanly of their fellows, and act
meanly towards them, and thereby they
grow mean and narrow in their own natures.
With no broad outlook upon human life and
duty, but wholly wrapt up in the mantle of
their own selfishness, they live on husks until
old age creeps upon them, and they find
themselves fattened with emptiness.   If there
is a pitiable thing in all this universe more
pitiable than another, it is a human being
nearing the land of shadows, with a heart
barren of generous impulses—a life crowned
by no starry garland of noble deeds.

Who that reasons—who that would live in

the upper story of his own marvelous being, and get the best out of life and its experiences—can look out upon Nature in her peaceful and gentle moods, and not feel her silent influence distilling like a sweet incense through all his soul?

Let us resolve to gather wisdom from all that we are and are a part of—from every surrounding circumstance and condition of life and death—laying up some golden stores of character, some precious treasures of soul, with every experience, against the bleak Winter whose outlying and bordering Springtime fills the measureless Beyond.

———●○◇▩◇○●———

As there is no such thing as equality among men in their capacity to master the conditions and bear the burdens of life, therefore government should recognize this fact and favor the weak horse in the team with the longer end of the whiffletree. In other words, the burdens of government should be made to rest upon the shoulders of those best able to bear them—which means graduated taxation.

MATERIALISM.

WITH the spread and growth of material-
ism in the world, coupled with the
increasing difficulties in the way of meeting
the demands of life—demands often fictitious
and exacting,—we find a growing disregard
for life itself.   And this is not at all surprising.
Without the hope of something beyond—a
reasonable assurance that this stage of existence does not bring us to the end of the
journey--the man overwhelmed with trouble,
and feeling himself no longer of any use in
the world, very naturally concludes that the
best disposition he can make of himself is to
quit, and close out his contract with existence. From his standpoint of thought he
reaches conclusions wholly in accordance
with the natural deductions of reason. But
does he not reason from false premises ?
Assuming that he does so reason there seems
to be a necessity for something to anchor
him more securely to life and duty ; and
there can be no anchor so firm as the as-

surance of another life. Such an assurance seems to carry with it an awakened sense of obligation to this life. It tells us that we have a work to do here, and that if we shirk that work in any way it will be worse for us there. And then it is the dread and uncertainty of the nature of that life—"what dreams may come when we have shuffled off this mortal coil, must give us pause," and induce us to stay by this life as long as possible.

We have no sympathy with that cold, calculating philosophy that robs man of all hope of a future life, and leaves him stranded on the bleak shores and shoals of time. It is then he becomes a fit subject for despair. Groping in the dark of his own obscured hopes he loses faith in himself. He turns his eyes earthward among the shadows and he sees no light in the gloaming—no beckoning hand in the distance. If he would only look the other way how changed would all things appear.

How often do we have occasion to say to some soul bowed down with a great sorrow, or overtaken by some great affliction, Be brave and strong, and don't give up the fight. What! surrender life, with all its possibilities of growth and grandeur. How much better to go down with face to the foe and with colors nailed to the mast.

And this is the spirit in which we should grapple with existence. If trouble comes— if foes to body or soul assail—place your back to the wall and face them bravely, determined to conquer or die trying. If they come of your own folly and inviting, the greater the need for prompt and decisive battle that shall leave you not only victor but wiser. With every effort to conquer there comes support from without and from within. There are Bluchers in reserve in every heart-struggle, ready at the word of command to hurl their legions upon the foe in your defence. Resolve to live, and live to some noble purpose. Never surrender, though the powers of earth and air combine against you, and hell yawns at your feet.

This is the path of duty, to watch and to wait, trusting the Good Father for what we can not clearly understand. Full soon will come the wintry frosts of age—the bowed form—the hesitating step—the trembling hand. Already, with many of us, the shadows are falling and lengthening toward the east, and the night cometh on apace. Let it not be a night of pitiless gloom, but one fringed with the glory of a coming day.

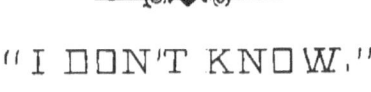

"I DON'T KNOW."

IT takes a large amount of knowledge, grounded in a solid substratum of common sense, to enable a man to say, "I don't know." There are so many people who claim to know, but who actually know so little or nothing of what they pretend, that it is indeed refreshing to meet, as we do occasionally, with a great, big-hearted, honest doubter—not one who doubts captiously and dogmatically ; but one who modestly doesn't know, and knows that he doesn't know, and isn't ashamed to own it.

All conscious human life is a stupendous interrogation point. It questions everything —the stars, the air, the earth, the sky. It looks down upon the blade of grass, the dew-drop sparkling in the sunbeam, the mole burrowing blindly under the ground, the beetle hiding among the clods, the corn ripening in the Autumn haze. It peers into the wondering, staring eyes of the new-born babe, and notes the far-off, vacant look of the dying. It sees wrong and sin reveling in luxury, and honest merit out at the knees and elbows. It dissects down through the tissues of the body, and searches among the secret springs and recesses of heart and brain. It traverses the realm of thought, emotion, passion, will. And it is eternally asking, Wherefore? Wherefore? What does all this mean? It coins its questions into verse :

Eternal Truth ! Oh, why does the wail
  Of the innocent burst in anguish sad ?
Oh, why does the wrong in pomp prevail,
  And the right in penury's rags go clad ?

Tell me, ye twinkling orbs of night,
  That jewel the skies with golden gems,
Do beings dwell in thy realms of light ?
  Are their brows encircled with diadems ?

Relentless Death, Oh why dost thou nip
  The tender flowers, the young and the fair,
And dash the cup from the spirit's lip,
  That the tempter, Hope, hath lifted there?

Thou mystic river, when time is o'er
  And we drift on thy dreary tide away,
Will our barks e'er reach the other shore?
  Will our spirits wake to a brighter day?

Will the phantoms of bliss that elude us here,
  And hopes that charm in their dazzling sheen,
Be ours to possess in that blissful sphere,
  With never a yawning gulf between?

And so we go on, ever questioning, and
hoping, and outreaching towards the light,
and wondering if the day will ever come
when we shall see and know. Thrice happy
he through whose inner consciousness comes
some satisfying answer, bringing with it an
abiding, restful trust—a voice that shall
break in waves of gladness over his doubting
soul, saying—

Perhaps ; but wait till this mortal night,
  With its shadows of doubt, shall fade away ;
All things shall seem in that better light
  As never they did in thy house of clay.

Then shall the vanishing hand of time
 Remove from thy heart all doubts and fears,
And the chastened soul to lights sublime,
 Shall rise from the mists of thy mortal years.

And in this faith we must rest—if not wholly content, at least we should school ourselves to be reasonably satisfied therewith, until we can obtain the better knowledge—till "faith shall be swallowed up in sight," and death shall be lost in victory.

Therefore we give joyful welcome and all hail to any system of religion or philosophy that helps to lift man out of his doubts, and to place his feet upon some rock of assurance —whether of faith or assumed knowledge— assurance in the satisfying belief in a hereafter ; that eternal progress is a law of being, and that the time will surely come when the labyrinthian maze of doubt and ignorance, through which we are groping here, shall open out into a way where we shall see all things clearly ; where all clouds shall disappear, all riddles shall be solved, and where we shall KNOW.

POWER OF LOVE.

F all the forces in the universe of spirit
or matter,—forces that play upon the
emotions, or actuate humanity in any way—
there is none so potential in its influence as
the all-conquering power of love. It is alike
the solace of tired hearts, and the motive
that moves the universe. How wonderful is
it in all its varied phases ;—parental and
conjugal love, that holds the world of humanity in its orbit, and makes existence
possible,—social and fraternal love, that
binds society into indissoluble bonds, making
existence tolerable,—self-love, that inspires
ambition, binding the higher loves into a
chain of strength and beauty, and making
them more effective in moulding and binding
character into lasting shapes of harmony and
grandeur.

The world would indeed be a stupendous
bear garden—a vast den of snarling mon-
sters, who would in the end devour each
other and become extinct,—but for this

magic balm from the pharmacy of heaven, distilling ever softly and gently among the sterner and baser purposes and passions of the soul, and the cruel and selfish instincts of undeveloped and unspiritualized human nature. It is as though the doors of Heaven had been left open, and from thence was wafted the fragrance of all joy and gladness to inspire humanity with the motives to a truer and diviner life. Show us the soul wherein love is not, and there we shall find one in which all the diviner chords of being are out of tune—a heart in which the baser impulses are found running riot and making sad havoc and inharmony with the entire being. There we shall find misanthropy souring and poisoning the sweet springs of life,—selfish greed trampling out gentle charity and even humanity's self,—unsated ambition that scruples at no means for the attainment of its ends,—anger, revenge, hatred—demons all—rankling in the sacred places of the soul, and making it a dismal cavern for the abode of unholy things.

Human life, however grand in intellect, or self-reliant in the majesty of its own powers, must have something to lean upon, especially in its hours of trial that come to all. Without some gentle outreaching of the affections ; without the clinging and twining of the heart's tendrils to and around some other life or lives, with its inflowing solace of compensating gladness, as the reward and counterpois of such tender outreachings and yearnings, life is indeed a dreary desert waste—a sky without a sun—a night without one smiling or redeeming star. It is then duty becomes a pathway of thorns to be trodden with aching heart and bleeding feet. The bright sunshine, the overarching sky, the melody of brooks and birds, the wooing of fragrant zephyrs, the myriad lips and forms of grand and glorious Nature, voice no sound of gladness to that gloomy soul. It moves on sadly and silently amid the shadows, until at last life itself grows to be a burden and a curse. But when love flashes its divine rays along the way, then every burden seems light, every task a living joy, and duty becomes a pathway strewn with flowers.

"A new commandment I give unto you," said the Great Teacher, "that ye love one

another." Here is the sum and substance
of all religion. It is the crown and glory of
manhood—the guerdon of life everlasting—
the shining pathway to the stars.

HEROISM IN COMMON LIFE.

E who leads a forlorn hope "into the
jaws of death," with the eyes of the
world resting upon him, is much less a hero
than he who, beset by the snares and temptations of life, triumphs over the evil promptings of his own nature. There is an unwritten heroism in common life that far excels
the storied heroism of the great and power-
ful. It costs one something to be brave and
true when no eye but the eye of one's own
soul rests upon him—when no approving
smile cheers him on save that of his own
conscience. And yet there are many such
heroes in all the silent and unheralded ways
of life.

We have seen a fair young girl, frail in
health, but brave and strong in purpose, turn

aside from the seductive allurements to a
frivolous and empty life—from the temptations to a luxurious and wicked one—and,
storing her mind with the treasures of knowledge, fit herself for a noble work and duty.
We have seen her take up her own and
others' burdens, and, oftimes with aching
heart and bleeding feet, bear them uncom-
plainingly along life's rugged way. We
have seen a young man, cast out upon the
world, homeless and friendless, but buoyant
in spirit, and exuberant with healthy life—
with mind and heart keenly sensitive to all
the fascinating pleasures that lure but to
destroy,—shutting himself out from the companionship of his kind, and setting his face
firmly against the enticements and besetting
snares of the world. We have seen him
" burning the midnight oil," and with eyes
fixed on the shining hights, laying deep and
broad the foundations of a character upon
which to rear the superstructure of a manhood that should withstand the "shocks of
time," the turmoil and vicissitudes of life,—
till old age should mantle it with its snows.
We have seen men and women in humble

life,—born to the hard conditions of poverty
and toil,—with hearts attuned to all goodness, and souls sweet with the refining baptism of unselfish charity. We have seen
them bending beneath their burdens of care,
of sickness, of poverty—with faces illumined
with the smile of God,—grand men and
noble women, whose unwritten life-histories
might be summed up in the words—" No
trust betrayed—no duty left undone."

Are not such as these the world's truest
heroes and heroines? And are not their
names deserving of enrollment on Fame's
whitest and most enduring scroll?

IN proportion as labor-saving machinery
supplements muscle in the work of the world
there will naturally be a decreasing demand
for labor unmixed with brains ; hence, the
laboring man should learn to master the
machine and not let the machine master him.

THE evil that some unbalanced natures do
is, doubtless, from their standpoint of reasoning, the right thing for them to do.

SOMETHING AND NOTHING

THE difference between having something and having nothing, is usually the difference between saving and wasting. There may be exceptional cases, arising from physical disability, or mental incapacity, but there are hardly enough of them to vitiate the rule.

It is indeed true that some people are born to wealth, and hence need not trouble themselves much about temporal things. It is a great misfortune to one to be thus born ; for he is denied the soul growth and strength that comes of striving. Rich men's sons are proverbial for their uselessness. Although they may inherit a very fair stock of elemental character, it is apt to be spoiled in the shaping. Society pampers and dawdles them, until they grow vain, proud, and conceited with an importance that they do not possess. And then, in the great world of work and use, they become of no more consequence than a Prince Charles poodle in the economy of a stag hunt. A man needs to struggle with the hard conditions of poverty to bring out the best there is in him. The world's masters and heroes of to-day—its men of brains and energy—sprung from humble beginnings.

But the great mass of mankind are born to toil ; and it is well they are, or in the onward sweep of time humanity would soon gravitate to the lower forms of life whence it sprung. It is to this toiling class—the bone and sinew of society—the honey-gatherers of life's busy hive—we wish to direct our "talk" to-day.

Why is it that we find so many people in the world without homes, or other earthly possessions—people of intelligence, culture, and of industrious habits. Many who have reached the meridian of life—good people— temperate people—lay by nothing from year to year against the rainy day of sickness, or the gray Winter of old age. Whatever their income they manage that it shall not exceed their outcome ; and they are generally to be found in a chronic condition of "hard up;" They evidently believe in having a good time as they go along. In a certain sense they are right; and yet, how much more of solid comfort could they not obtain out of life if they only managed, during their years of earnings, however humble, to lay by something for a sung little home they could call their own.

There is no poor man, of ordinary industry, but that has his times of prosperity. He obtains a good paying job, occasionally, or enjoys a season of extra remunerative wages. But instead of improving the occasion as a starter for a home, it is made the means for a larger measure of present gratification.

A hard-working mechanic will frequently squander for beer and tobacco, or in some other foolish gratification, a whole day's earnings; and his wife will make herself wretched if she can't have as nice a bonnet as is worn by the wife of old Moneygrubs across the way. It isn't so much what a man earns or spends that makes or breaks him, as it is what he saves. It is his determination always to calculate upon a little margin for the family sinking fund, which shall be sacred from spoliation.

Poor people, with nothing to depend upon for a subsistence but the labor of their hands, are foolishly blind to their own truest happiness when they seek to imitate the follies of the wealthy. It can only be done at a sacrifice of that independence of character and individuality of manhood and womanhood which constitute the bulwark and casemate of every individual soul.

When a man has learned to live within his means, and lay by a trifle for emergencies, even though he has to wear his coat out at the elbows and his shoes out at the toes, and can snap his fingers in the face of society and say, "I don't care for your nonsense," he becomes a moral hero of whom the world should be proud. And the woman who, in her own sweet simplicity, can wear a calico dress, and be happy and independent, while her next door neighbor indulges in silks, has mastere d one of the most difficult problems of existence. God bless such people, say we. We wish there were more of that kind in the world.

Not that we would disparage any adornment that adds to the beauty and symmetry of "the house we live in"—the divine temple of the human soul. But it should be done from a love of the beautiful in one's own soul, rather than from any vain desire to shine in the eyes of a foolish world. And then such adornments should always be made secondary to comfort; and never should they be indulged in beyond what one's means will reasonably warrant, nor at the expense of that peace of mind, without which all else is a hollow mockery.

—————

THE amount of vitality wasted by young men in smoking cigarettes, would, if properly applied, enable them to lay such lasting foundations of character as would give them a prominent place among the world's heroes, statesmen, orators, poets, painters, lawgivers, and even editors. But as it is they smoke away their brains and turn out noodles.

WE often commit a great mistake in withholding our good opinions of those we love until after they are dead, and then inscribing upon their tombstones the approving words their hearts hungered for while living.

OLD AGE.

WHERE is no sight more beautiful than that of a man or woman who has passed the meridian of life, with locks whitening in the frosts of years, and with face turned towards the setting sun, growing old sweetly and gracefully. There ought to be no such thing as old age, except in a physical sense. Years should bring wisdom to the mind, and growth and grandeur to the soul, but not age to the heart. That should be kept ever young and fair. It should become more and more beautiful and fragrant with Spring blossoms as the years roll away.

But there is so much to make us old in spirit—so many cares and heart-aches, so much work and worry, so many losses and disappointments—that we grow old and tired, and lose our youthful freshness and fragrance, oftentimes, ere we are aware.

In the morning of life our ships sail away to unknown seas, well ballasted with hope and ambition. We reck not that a thousand dangers await them. They encounter storm and tempest, fierce cyclones, treacherous currents, sunken rocks. Unless staunch and true, and well manned with a resolute crew, they soon become drifting wrecks, or go down beneath the engulfing waves. How few return to us freighted with the rich invoices of character which constitute the soul's true wealth. We sought for earthly treasures—treasures of worldly gain, social position, gratified ambition—and our ships return to us empty laden. And then the shadows of disappointment and blighted hopes gather over us and turn the fresh Springtime of our lives into cheerless Autumn. It is thus we grow old, wrinkled, and gray, in spirit, and the outlook grows darker as we near the end.

The end? Rather should we not say the beginning? And what a beginning! But even were this life the all in all of being, and there were no individualized conscious existence beyond, then how sad and unsatisfactory indeed would be such an ending. Why, if we lived as we ought—if we made our ventures cautiously, and with a view to those imperishable treasures of heart and soul that survive the ravages of time, instead of seeking so entirely after the fleeting and fading things of earth,—life would grow richer and sweeter as the evening advances and its shadows lengthen. Profiting by every experience—by every burden and heart-ache, every mistake and failure,—we would gather strength and beauty with our years, and then we should approach the goal as calmly and softly—

> " As fades the Summer cloud away,
>   As sinks the gale when storms are o'er,
> As gently shuts the eye of day,
>   And dies the wave along the shore."

It takes but really little to make a man happy, if he only knows it! The trouble with most people is they don't know it. They imagine that certain factitious circumstances in life—certain wealthy conditions and surroundings ; the ability to outshine and outrival in the hollow mockery of life, fashionable society ; that these are the cargoes our ships should bring back in order to give us happiness. There never was a graver mistake. True happiness must come from within, and it needs but little from without to make it reasonably complete.

When this lesson is well learned and profited by, then are we but prepared to live. Then shall we know no such thing as age, save in that gentle decay of physical life that even adds a charm and a zest to the higher enjoyments of the soul. And thus it is that when this life is most complete that we are best prepared to lay it down and take our chances with what follows—confidently believing that if it is truly well with us here it will be all right with us there.

<hr>

THE man or woman who has no well spring of joy within—no resources of philosophy whence to derive consolation when trouble comes—has failed to profit by the hard lessons of life.

As THE child can not learn to walk without some stumbling, neither can there be any soul-growth without some mistakes ; so it is better to grow and stumble than never to grow at all.

NATURE

NATURE, in her varying moods, is to day a merciless tyrant, and anon a gentle and loving mother. We look upon the track where the fierce cyclone has spent its fury, leaving death and destruction in its path ; we mark the wrecks that bestrew the shore when the wrath of the waves has subsided ; we look down into the pleading eyes of the dying babe ; and in all this apparent inharmony we can discover naught but cruelty—cruelty without a motive, without one redeeming trait. If there is an intelligent purpose in Nature—a guiding hand in the universe, that holds the stars in their course, and commands the elements to do its bidding,—as we are taught to believe, and as no mortal can wisely deny,—why, we ask in vain of our own souls, was this violence and cruelty necessary ? Why are the elements permitted to rend and lay waste ? Why the blighting winds to sap the budding harvests, that famine and death may ravish

the homes of the poor? Why is helpless
infancy and inoffensive manhood made to
endure the torture and anguish of affliction,
while multitudes less worthy are permitted
to live upon the mountain top of health and
happiness?

Again, we look abroad in the world, and
behold, where lately swept the mad cyclone
the wild flower now turns its gentle face to
the sun, and the bobolink builds its nest in
the fragrant grass ; where the billows, lashed
into madness by the fierce tempest, hurled
the venturesome sailor to swift destruction,
the cooing ripples now kiss the white pebbles
at our feet ; and from the pillow of anguish,
where pain and suffering long held high car-
nival among the nerves of helpless innocence,
there now distills the precious balm of roseate
health, and the child walks forth again to
blissful companionship with the birds and
flowers.

We can not understand these things.
They are beyond our reach ; and it were
vain to try to reconcile them with our narrow
ideas of the eternal fitness of things. They
must forever remain among those hidden

problems concerning which we can only speculate, and the solution of which, if ever, must be when man has "climbed the golden stair," to hights of wisdom and intelligence vastly beyond that which he now occupies.

We must accept the fact of Nature, with all her apparent cruelty and injustice, and it were folly to complain. Isn't it really better to think that what is incomprehensible to us in our present state, will sometime or other be made clear; that Nature's seeming indifference to us, and even her apparent mistakes and cruelties, are all parts of some plan and purpose, which, if rightly understood, would seem divinely grand and beautiful? May it not be that the storm and the tempest, the lightning and the earthquake, are essential to the unfoldment of Nature's truer harmonies, or even to the existence of life itself; that sorrow, suffering and death, are all important factors in the problem of life and happiness; and that when the veil shall fall from our eyes and the clouds shall lift from our souls, we shall learn to realize that it is all for the best.

Ought we not to school our minds to this

faith, while at the same time we are ever endeavoring to discover what Nature means, and seeking to know more and more of her secret mysteries? In this faith we believe life may be made to yield its best results, and human duty will become a pathway strewn with flowers.

AGREEING TO DISAGREE.

S we have somewhere said in these "Talks," people differ most concerning those things of which they know the least ; and, generally they really wrangle and quarrel only about what they positively know nothing. The subject is worthy of further consideration.

A demonstrated fact admits of no controversy. No intelligent persons ever quarrel about the sphericity of the earth, or the law of gravitation that holds the planets in their courses. There was a time when, with less knowledge, they were ready to

break each other's heads over all such propositions. As knowledge increased in the
world the once common causes of disagreement disappeared, and new and more remote
causes appeared, and are continually appear-
ing, so that there is seemingly no end to
the subject.

It is doubtless a part of the great plan
that man shall have something to quarrel
about, otherwise he would never arrive at
truth. It is the nature of unfolding intellect
to seek controversy. Without the attrition
of mind with mind resulting therefrom there
would be no intellectual growth. Man
would stagnate and relapse into a condition
of mental torpor scarcely in advance of that
of the brute. The trouble with him is to
discriminate between the knowable and the
unknowable, in the matters he is disposed to
differ about ; and yet, perhaps, the very
lack of such discrimination is his salvation.
Otherwise his capacity for knowledge would
be circumscribed and his intellectual powers
dwarfed thereby.

Man must forever be reaching outward
and upward into the realm of causes—ever

grappling with the secret problems of nature and of his own existence—no matter whether the solution of said problems is within his grasp or not. To give up trying to solve them would be to be false to his own divine, outreaching nature.

Therefore, the central thought which we desire to impress upon the minds of all who find in these " Talks " any food for reflection, is, that we should gracefully accept the fact of our many and varied phases of disagreement—in other words, that we should "agree to disagree," and make the best of it. We should endeavor to realize, in thinking our neighbors fools for not believing as we do, that they, likewise, are sure that we are fools for not seeing things in their light.

We should endeavor to appreciate the fact that belief is the result of conditions of mind not always under the control of the judgment,—religious belief especially, which deals, of necessity, more or less with the unknowable. The fact should make us charitable and tolerant of the opinions of others. It should teach us our insignificance as factors in the universe of souls. It should cause us, in the domain of uncertainties, to feel our way cautiously. It should divest us of all dogmatism and narrowness of soul, and improve, refine and ennoble our ways of thought.

Thus shall we grow in those intellectual and spiritual graces which adorn and exalt manhood, and bring us nearer and nearer unto the likeness of the Divine.

ONE true friend, to whom you can go for sympathy and succor in your hour of sorest need, and feel in your soul that your dearest confidence will never be betrayed, is worth more to you than a million sunshine flatterers, who fawn and smile, and dance around you, in the days of your prosperity.

WHEN the Great Teacher said, "It is easier for a camel to go through the eye of a needle than for a rich man to enter into the kingdom of God," he probably knew what he was saying. At the same time he doubtless never intended to be understood as intimating that there was any virtue in poverty.

THERE is a beautiful eastern legend that has found expression in many languages. It relates that Sandalphon, the Angel of Light and Glory, standing at the gates of the Celestial City, gathers the fervent prayers and heart-longings of sorrowing humanity, as they ascend ; they are turned to flowers in his hands, and their fragrance is wafted throughout the abode of the immortals. A faithful and striking allegory this of a great law of compensation in human suffering.

While "sickness and sorrow, pain and death," is the common lot of mortals; yet some there be who seem born to more than their share of ills—if that may be called ill, which, in the process of spiritual unfoldment, becomes a means of growth and strength. There are some natures so finely tuned, and so sensitive to the discords and inharmonies of life, that they suffer keenly from causes that would scarcely disturb the equanimity of others. They feel the rough blasts, and shrink from the cutting frosts, when hardier and tougher natures would withstand the shock with scarcely a sense of weakness. One is a sturdy oak—the granite rock ; the other the sensitive plant—the fragile, but rare and sparkling crystal.

Nature's estimate of the value of a man is his capacity for suffering, and the effect that suffering has upon him. If it fails to sweeten, purify, and ennoble his life, it is because l.e is composed of base metal, which turns into dross in the furnace heat of affliction. This is the diamond drill that tests the value of the entire lode of human character. It is the ladder that reaches to the skies, up whose shining hights all true souls are ever ascend- ing. Suffering is as essential to soul-growth as earthly food is to the development of the physical body. The heart that has never been bent to the rack, nor felt the lacerating thong of some great sorrow, has missed the emblazoned way to true happiness. " For our light affliction," says St. Paul, " which is but for a moment, worketh for us a far more exceeding and eternal weight 'of glory." And thus the sorrows of the present become the joys of the future—are turned to flowers in the hands of the good angel that waits for us at the pearly gateway of the skies.

The common mishaps, troubles and sorrows of life, have their uses in harrowing and fertilizing the soul, and thereby preparing it for a better harvest of good thoughts and noble deeds,—just as the farmer upon virgin soil oftentimes finds it necessary to destroy the brambles and weeds by fire in order to prepare the land for the blessed corn. Human life needs fallowing with a keen plowshare to prepare it for the golden harvest— the luscious fruitage. And the richer the soil the greater the necessity for careful and thorough culture, to guard against the rank growth of hurtful things ever ready to creep in and choke out the precious plants.

What tired and patient soul, approaching the gentle rest of death, with calm resignation and unclouded trust, and looking back over a life of many cares and sorrows, but feels to rejoice in every pang it has suffered —in every tear it has shed? It would not, if it could, have borne or endured a single sorrow or heart-ache less. Even in this life,

with all grand souls, do not their trials and
struggles turn to flowers, exhaling the sweet
fragrance of beautiful thoughts to bless and
enrich the world?

Of all grand inspirations of genius that
have marked the eras of human history, and
left their impress upon the monumental
records of time—in literature, art, song, invention,—the grandest and best have been
born of heart-throes of which the world has
little dreamed. From altars where souls
have bled, and brows have been pierced
with crowns of cruel thorns, have leapt forth
lightnings that have thrilled the world, and
marked a shining pathway for other feet to
follow. From Gethsemanes of anguish and
tears have been voiced lessons of charity, of
gentle humanity and love, that have awakened
slumbering echoes in benighted souls, the
world over, that shall reverbrate through all
time.

Tired hearts, suffering souls, ye who have
borne the burdens of cruel wrongs, and
trodden the thorny ways of the world with
bleeding feet, take heart and hope in the
thought that the time will surely come when

your troubles will all be turned to flowers, whose joyful fragrance shall exhale in blessings and gladness forevermore.

JOB'S QUERY.

IN all ages of the world intelligent humanity everywhere has puzzled its brain over Job's query: "If a man die, shall he live again?" And, as in the science, philosophy and religion of his day, Job found no answer to his question, and was inclined to believe, with "the Preacher," that in aught that pertained to an existence beyond this life, "man hath no pre-eminence above a beast;" so, a vast multitude of the sons of earth, to-day, are disposed to accept Job's view of the matter, and with him to say: "As the waters fail from the sea, and the flood decayeth and dryeth up, so man lieth down and riseth not: till the heavens be no more, they shall not awake nor be raised out of their sleep."

It is claimed by the materialist that the idea of continued existence is the outgrowth of education ; that the desire for such existence is unnatural, and has no place in the mind, except as it is implanted there by erroneous teaching. And nature, at the first thought, seems to bear him out in his conclusions. We find man and the higher forms of life below him, to be very nearly the same in physical structure. There is the same muscular, arterial, osseous and nervous systems. The blood is of the same color, and it is re-charged with oxygen in the same way. Life is sustained by the same process in the one as in the other. And then, leaving the domain of the physical, he finds much in the mental nature that is similar in kind—affection, memory, locality, calculation ; and sometimes he finds manifestations of intelligence trenching so closely upon the human that it is difficult to define the difference.

Following this strictly physical and mental similarity between the so-called dumb brute and the human being, the scientific materialist points us to types of savage life scarcely a

grade above the higher simious forms, and the
believer in immortality, by faith or otherwise,
is puzzled with the question, " At what point
in the scale of being does the capacity for
immortality begin?" Other perplexing
questions arise as to the nature of that part
or element of man for which religion claims
an eternity of existence. Is it an individualized entity? Has it shape, memory, passion,
will? Where does it dwell and how does it
exist? In short, what is it? And then if
man only is immortal, would not the hunter
be lost without the companionship of his
faithful hound—the Arab without his trusty
steed?

It would be entirely foreign to our purpose
in these "Talks" to attempt any elaborate
disquisition upon these or any other questions. We aim rather to catch a few practical and pointed thoughts on each theme we
attempt to consider, and impinge the same
upon the consciousness of our readers—not
always so much by way of instruction as to
arouse thought in their minds.

Now there is no intelligent materialist but
will admit that there are phases and phenom-

ena of mind which are entirely inexplicable upon any known theory of the laws of matter, and which certainly strongly indicate that this life is not the all of being.   Take, for instance, the fact of somnambulism, showing the operation of mind independent of its usual channels of communication ; mesmerism, demonstrating the power of one mind over the mind and body of another, operating, often, at long distances ; clairvoyance, clairaudience, and the various and well attested phenomena of modern spiritualism, all "footfalls on the boundaries of another world," and pointing to an almost positive affirmation of Job's question.

And then again, admitting that the desire for continued existence is the result of education, the capacity for such educated desire inheres only in man, and not at all, as far as we know, in types of animal life below man Because man desires immortality may be no evidence or argument that his desire will ever be gratified.   At the same time, we notice, that in the material world nature aims to perfect whatever she undertakes.   Why should she leave her grandest work—the intellectual and spiritual nature of man—all incomplete, with its longings and outreachings all unsatisfied, its unfoldment but just begun? Man lives here but a little while, learns some few things imperfectly, and is cut off just upon the threshold of that development that he feels he is capable of, and ought, in the purposes of his being, to be allowed to accomplish. Denied this, he feels that he would be made an unfair exception to the creative law of the universe, and he rebels against the thought in every atom of his being.

But, whether man lives again, or not, he is tolerably sure of an existence here. He should make the most of his present opportunities, and get all the good out of life he possibly can ; and this can be done only by doing the greatest possible amount of good to others.

———⧫———

MOTHERS who worry and fret, and scold and borrow trouble, about what they can not help, only make themselves miserable, without securing any compensating benefit.

NOT TO BE WONDERED AT,

IT is not to be wondered at that men and women, with keenly sensitive natures, often become cynical and morose, if not wholly disgusted with, and tired of the world. There is so much to worry and annoy such natures—so much inharmony and rasping discord to contend with, that they find themselves incapable of bearing up under the burdens of life. Especially is this the case where they are obliged, for physical sustenance, to enter the lists in the competitive struggle for bread. To be jostled against and misunderstood by coarser natures, pushed aside and crowded to the wall by brawnier muscle, and to see the morsel that should have been theirs seized upon and devoured by the grasping and greedy crowd, is not calculated to sweeten one's disposition —unless one is so schooled in the philosophy of life as to be able to accept all things for the best.

Life is too short to enable the most thought-

ful mind to fully comprehend the situation—
to take in and realize, much less to analyze,
its relations with the universe and with itself.
Man opens his eyes for a little while on a
wonderful panorama of field and sky, of
ocean and desert, of marvelous manifestations of intelligence and strange conflicts of
ideas. He finds himself a conscious and
sentient entity—an atom clinging to a
globule of condensed nebulæ, whirling through
the mighty voids of space. His abode is
one of the least of untold millions of similar
globes, and for aught he knows he may be
least among the vast hosts of conscious atoms
peopling the same. He opens his eyes upon
all these marvels, catches but a bare glance
of things, and then the curtain falls, the show
is ended, and the spectator goes to his long
home.

In all this brief and flitting glance,—but
nevertheless to the man of thought and culture, a broad and comprehensive view of
the universe of mind and matter,—and especially in his apparent littleness, and in the
inferior quality of his fellow atoms, he sees
and realizes his own insignificance in the

great universal plan, and he is led to exclaim with Job, " What is man that Thou shouldst be mindful of him?" This sense of littleness and inferiority—a feeling all unknown except to truly noble souls—is apt to prey upon a sensitive nature until the man actually comes to think that he is of no possible account in the world ; and then, when brought into disagreeable and unavoidable contact with rude and ignoble natures, as he inevitably must be, the result is often more than he can bear. He loses his grip, as it were, and misses the glorious opportunity for spiritual and intellectual unfoldment which life affords.

We pity the soul who finds no joy in the world—who sees only the shadows, and never basks in the glorious sunshine. It is a soul out of tune with the real harmonies of nature. For though nature has its dark sides—its clashing inharmonies,—it has also its realms of gladness—its divine melodies. And misguided indeed is that man or woman who dwells perpetually in the one, and never seeks out or learns the joys of the other.

We insist that the true theory of life is to make the most and best of it, under all circumstances and all conditions. To endeavor to right the wrongs of society, to help the "weary and heavy laden" on his way, to speak the gentle word that carries peace and rest to the troubled soul, to bless the widow and the fatherless in their affliction, to admonish the erring in the spirit of charity and love, to make the moral wastes of the world to blossom as the rose,—in all this and more, man can find no time to grow cynical or sour—no moment when he may not be adding to the stature and glory of his own manhood, and fitting himself more and more for that life which we believe will bourgeon and blossom for him "within the vail," forevermore.

As man ascends the scale of being he will take less and less delight in all sports or pastimes that inflict pain upon dumb brutes. He will find his enjoyments in those higher delights of the soul that exalt even as they gratify.

TAXATION without representation is as great a wrong to woman as it ever was to man.

AFTER ALL.

SOCIETY is so accustomed to weigh men by their success in acquiring property that many a man counts his life a failure who, dying, leaves no stores of earthly treasures for his heirs to quarrel over. Never was there a greater mistake. A man's coin value is really his lowest and meanest value. Wealth is often his ruination, generally his curse, and always a source of annoyance and care. The acquisition of a reasonable amount of property—enough to ward off the possibility of want in old age—is both desirable and commendable. But that once obtained, and absolutely assured, life, surely, has other objects that are infinitely nobler than the continued piling up of wealth. Many a man, with the acquisitive faculty largely developed, gathers in wealth for the purpose of doing good with it, and after scattering kindness and sunshine all along his path, manages to come out about even in the end. Such a man has lived to some purpose, and we doubt not has got out of life more solid happiness in each month of his existence than ever Moneybags obtained from his dollars in his whole lifetime. The only true measurement of a man and the highest standard of his valuation, is character. If he bears about him the genuine article stamped and registered in the mint of true manhood, he is rich, and never otherwise. Many of the greatest benefactors of the world—the master minds whose names will go down to remotest time —never had time to acquire worldly riches ; and yet they are the Rothchilds, Stewarts and Astors, of the world of soul. What is the use, then, of wasting one's best energies for what one really does not need? For after all, life is a success or failure only in proportion to its accumulation of those treasures of heart and brain that endure forever.

If the acquisitive faculty was the highest faculty of the human brain Providence would have located it in the arch of the temple, and not crowded it off among combativeness, secretiveness, and the other animal faculties.

HARMLESS SELF-CONCEIT.

THERE are many excellent people in
the world who will confidently tell us
such amazing things of Deity—of His majesty,
power, purposes, laws,—and have such confidence in their ability to influence or per-
suade Him in matters that He might possibly
overlook or forget,—that one would naturally
conclude they must be on terms of peculiar
intimacy with the Creator. This is a harm-
less species of self-conceit, so long as it is
dominated by a sincere desire for the highest
welfare of humanity. We care but little
what kind of theology a man believes in,
provided he is actuated and permeated by
genuine love for his fellow men. He may
claim that the universe was created in six
days or six thousand æons ; he may locate
the time and place, and believe that the human race obtained its start by a special
creation of a perfect pair in the Garden of
Eden, or that it ascended, by the slow pro-

cess of evolution, from a mollusk or a monkey; he may think he knows that the first created pair fell from their high and holy estate through the wiles of a mischievous being who succeeded in circumventing his and their Creator; he may believe all this, and as much more, or less, as he can find it in his nature to believe; but if his heart is warm with the divine impulse of good will to man, he is our friend and brother. We have no quarrel with him. Indeed we can respect his opinions for his sake, and for the good there is in him.

But independent of all this assumed knowledge, and all of the marvelous riddles and hidden things of the universe, concerning which we can only speculate and theorize, there are some important facts—all-important for humanity to know—that are plainly within the reach of human knowledge. We know there is a life principle permeating matter, and pushing upward and outward into countless forms. Whether this principle inheres in, and is a property of, matter, solely, or is a something behind and independent of matter, is not essential to our welfare or happiness. The central fact of the existence of such a principle can no more be questioned than we can question the fact of our own existence.

In the operations of this principle, or law of matter, as some prefer to term it, we notice that it is ever reaching out through nature for the best. It is never satisfied with inferiority or mediocrity ; but, through all the countless cycles of time, is ever experimenting, as it were, and trying and retrying to produce something better and better. The air we breathe has undergone wonderful changes, since the earlier geologic eras, and is capable of sustaining vastly superior forms of life now to what it could then. This is. evident from the crude and extinct forms of vegetable and animal life folded away in the coal and chalk beds, or that have left their impress in the older rocks.

We trace humanity back along the line of human history until we see man emerging from the mists and shadows of antiquity, a mere savage, brutal and ignorant—a dweller in caves, and clad in the skins of wild beasts —whose highest ambition was carnage and conquest. We see him to-day crowned with the garnered wisdom of the past, sitting as king over new realms of thought, with the prisoned vapors of the cloud and the tamed coursers of the storm obedient to his call. Hence, we would conclude that man is no exception to Nature's progressive law—that he is undergoing a process of intellectual and spiritual growth and unfoldment that is limited and circumscribed only by eternity on the one side, and his own infinite capacity on the other.

Realizing this fact, and that Nature is ever calling to man by her myriad voices to come up higher—to ascend the scale of being to a companionship with his higher ideals—what sort of beings ought we to be? Who, with such possibilities before him, would be content to grovel in the muck and mire of an ignoble life, and feed on husks and garbage, when he has but to put forth his hand to pluck the golden fruits of paradise?

A SWEET disposition, in man or woman, is a jewel outshining the rarest of earthly gems.

PARENTAL GOVERNMENT.

———

TRAIN up a child in the way he should
go," said the wise man, "and when he
is old he will not depart from it." That
depends somewhat, Solomon, on the kind of
child you undertake to train up. We have
seen children, under the most strict and careful training, go to the bad in spite of every
wholesome restraint; while others, who
have come up without much of any training,
have turned out to be good and useful men
and women. Thus, we believe a great deal depends upon the inherited tendencies and qualities of the child, as to whether or not it will
walk in the way it is trained to go. It is a
well understood law of nature that like begets
like, and that children are very apt to inherit
the moral weaknesses and imperfections of
their progenitors, and especially are they apt to
be endowed with inharmonious and badly organized natures as the results of the ignorance or indifference of the parents concerning

the laws governing the ante-natal conditions of life. .

No man or woman bearing the taint of scrofula or consumption in their blood, or who can not control their own natural tendencies to evil, should ever reproduce their kind,—no man addicted to the intemperate use of liquor, opium or tobacco,—no thief, nor gambler, nor murderer ;—unless they would perpetuate their own evil propensities in the world, and add to the sum of human misery.

Now, as to the training up of children in the way they should go : The first and most important qualification is for the parents to take Josh Billings' advice and "go that way themselves." The proper method of correcting. children is one most difficult to learn. The nature and temper of the child must be thoroughly understood ; for what will benefit one may ruin another. The rod is a necessary implement of family government only with those parents who do not know how to govern by better and higher methods. The old adage, "spare the rod and spoil the child," had its origin in an age of semi-barbarism, and in a false idea of parental discipline. Many a boy, driven away from his home by parental cruelty, has gone forth into the world with all filial love crushed out of his heart. The blow that arouses anger, or deadens the love of a child for a parent, is an unfortunate one, and should never be given. No child, with any proper degree of spirit, and a fair amount of intelligence, that has arrived at years bordering on manhood or womanhood, will tamely submit to physical chastisement. Of course there may be natures so barren of the better promptings and impulses of humanity, that the infliction of physical pain is the shortest way to their consciousness. But even in such cases we seriously question whether the shortest is the best way.

The most successful horse-trainers are those who make the least possible use of the whip. The mind of the young child may be influenced in like manner, by gentle persuasion. Before arriving at years of discretion, it may be encouraged by rewards in ways of well doing, and checked by gentle restraints from its perverse purposes. The

children of parents who use the rod un-
sparingly, and who do not run away from
home as soon as they are able to take care
of themselves, are generally noted for their
stupidity and worthlessness.

The family bond of union should embrace
every member of the household. Children
should be made to realize that in all the wide
world their parents are their best friends.
They should learn to confide in them, and to
love their homes. But it is only the outreaching, tender hand of parental love that
can call forth this love in the child. Anger,
petulance, fault-finding and cruelty, will
never do it. Mothers who scold and fret,
and fathers who beat and bruise, surely can
not realize the mischief they are doing.

If a son or a daughter manifests a disposition to go astray, take them, father,
mother, to your loving arms and heart, and
gently and tenderly teach them the better
way. If this will not save them nothing on
earth will. The memory of your tender care
and loving counsels they will never forget
It will cling to them through all their future
years, like the whispered words of a dying

mother's prayer,—ever prompting and guiding them in the right whenever their wayward feet would go astray.

Here is the secret of all true parental government. And it is this principle that constitutes the chief factor in all human reform.
It is Omnipotent love working through
humanity. It is the key to heaven.

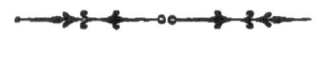

SUNSET.

THERE is no more suggestive or beautiful
sight, to our eyes, than that of an elderly
married couple, who, trustingly and lovingly,
together have walked the rugged ways of
life, from youth to old age ; and now, hand
in hand, and heart to heart, are patiently
and hopefully waiting upon the hither shore
of time for the sound of the boatman's oar,
that shall bear them across the silent river.

We look back along the dim vista of years
to the halcyon time of life's sunny morning.
We witness their plighted vows at the altar,

and see them go forth, in the pride and glory of their young wedded lives, to the toils and struggles of existence. Many a Godspeed and kind word of cheer fall upon their ears, as they go out from beneath the parental roof-tree that is to shelter them no more forever. Before them lies a new world of experiences—of joys and sorrows—of grand successes, and perhaps of sad failures. But strong of purpose and resolute of will, and with life's sky rose-tinted with the flush of dawn, they move on, and enter upon this, to them, all unexplored world of experiences.

We see them later established in their new home. Perhaps it is a log cabin in the wilderness, with neighbors few and far ; or maybe a cosy little cottage in some distant town. The husband is bravely bending every energy to the task of mastering the hard conditions of life—of carving out a home and a name in the world, and securing, if possible, that independence that shall relieve them from the possibility of want. To the wife's once rosy cheeks has come the pallor of the dreadful agonies of maternity ; but

now her eyes are bright with a new hope, as
she caresses the tiny form that nestles in her
bosom.

And then come added cares and heart-
aches as the years glide away. I see them,
with streaming eyes and pleading lips, bending over the couch of their darling one, as
its little life flutters away in the short gasps
of dissolution, and its eyes grow dim under
the touch of Death's icy fingers.   But
anon, time pours its gentle balm into their
wounded hearts, and the bitter trial and loss,
which they thought they could never endure,
fades away into a tender memory.

Again we behold them, and as in the long
ago they went forth into the world, now
their own noble sons and daughters, bur-
dened with the unsolved problems and un-
tried responsibilities of life, follow in their
footsteps ; and soon their home is left unto
them desolate, save in the companionship of
their own chastened souls.   Well for them
now if they find within themselves treasures
of culture and character that shall supply
their dearest need.   Well for them, if
schooled in that beautiful philosophy that

enabled St. Paul to say : "I have fought a good fight, I have finished my course, I have kept the faith," they, too, can feel in their souls that they have done the best they knew, and that now they will trust the good Father for all that is to come.

The shadows stretch away in lengthening lines toward the east; and now they are calmly watching the glories of the coming sunset—the sunset of a well-spent life. How grand they seem, in the fruition of their years, with their silvered hair glowing in the sunset's golden gleam. Their faces are radiant with a divine hope that beyond the bars of the shining west the beckoning arms of their loved ones are outreaching towards them to welcome them to their home of eternal rest and love ; and that in a few more days, or years at most, they will pass on, as one, weary with the burdens of the day, "gathers the drapery of his couch about him, and lies down to pleasant dreams."

IT doesn't hurt a good wife to praise her occasionally.

A DAY OF REST.

"BLESSED be the man that invented sleep," said Sancho Panza; but thrice blessed he, say we, who invented Sunday. To be able, for one glad day in seven, to cast aside all business care, and to find a brief surcease from the turmoil, the excitements and the worry of life, is surely a priceless boon to humanity, and one that the great Christian world does not fully appreciate.

While we are no Sabbatarian in the religious sense of the word—believing that all days alike are holy, as Nature is holy, and that all are made for the profit and unfoldment of halting, struggling, and yet really progressive humanity,—still we are deeply grateful for the institution of the Christian Sunday. And for the sake of those who especially venerate the day, and for our own sakes, we would make it as free from all secular pursuits as possible. Neither would we permit any who choose to devote the day to pleasurable enjoyment in any manner to disturb the quiet and religious devotion of those who believe that a special sanctity attaches thereto.

Of course there are many necessary pursuits of life where the observance of Sunday as a day of entire cessation from physical labor is either impossible, or would work a serious detriment to the laudable work of the world,—such as the navigation of the high seas, railroading, and many mechanical pursuits where cessation of labor would work serious waste.

And here we see and recognize the fitness of the idea that "Sunday was made for man," —that is, in the nature of things, the day must necessarily be made flexible to fit the inexorable and unyielding circumstances of humanity. These exceptions to the observance of Sunday should cause no uneasiness to religious people, and do not with those of any breadth of thought. They need not have the slightest apprehension that the day will ever be turned into one of general business, or lost in the whirl or waste of the world. It trenches too closely on man's necessities ever to be cast aside. On the other hand, it will grow upon the world just in proportion as society becomes enlightened, and the improving conditions of humanity will permit.

And so, while we may not fully subscribe to the reason of the pious poet for rejoicing for the gift of the Christian Sabbath, nevertheless we are not so bigoted as to be unwilling to join with him in the glad refrain—

> " Welcome sweet day of rest—
>   That saw the Lord arise;
>   Welcome to this reviving breast,
>   And these rejoicing eyes."

THE pampered daughter of luxury who turns up her nose at an honest, industrious mechanic, or worthy laborer of any kind, may see the time when a five dollar gold piece will look bigger to her than a cart wheel.

THE man, in this age, who selfishly lives for himself alone, was born ten thousand years too late.

TO the young man just entering upon the stage of active life, and who ought to be forming a character that shall constitute a sinking fund against the emergencies of life and the ravages of time, we have a few words to say.

In the first place, my young friend, you must learn the hard lesson that if ever you expect to amount to anything in life you must work for it. If nature has given you a capacious brain, that is your good luck, for which you should be thankful. You should modestly accept the gift, and set yourself at the task of improving the same. Nature turns out her diamonds always in the rough. The polishing and cutting are the work of man. On the other hand, if Nature has been less bountiful with you, then the greater the necessity for harder work. Many an inferior quality of brain, by energetic application, has been made to evolve a high order of manhood.

You should first endeavor to find out what you were intended for, and then direct all your energies in that direction. Many a good mechanic has been spoiled under the mistaken notion that he was best fitted for a professional life ; and many a fine brain has been deprived of advantages that, if properly improved upon, would have given a genius to the world. And once on the right track turn neither to the right nor the left ; and above all, work—work early and late—work with a will that will brook no denial or defeat.

He who would win must struggle for the prize. He can find no time for idleness, dissipation or folly. He is supplied with a certain amount of vitality—none too much. He has not a particle to waste in foolishness of any kind. Are you aware, my friend, that the cigarette to which you seem so devoted, uses up fully ten per cent of your vital force—of your capital stock of energy ? It deadens the resolution in your will, paralyzes your nerves, and relaxes your grip, as it were. Throw it away, and resolve that forever more you will be master of the situation, and that no such untidy or debilitating habit shall hold you captive at its feet. And then your occasional dissipations and late hours, they consume another large percentage of your vitality ; and ere you are aware you find a habit of indolence and indifference stealing over you, and your ventures bring you no return.

"But," do you ask, "would you deny young people all recreation—all pleasure?" By no means ; but we would have you to realize that there is no true pleasure in aught that hurts or degrades. Work may be made a pleasure and a joy when it leads to success. An earnest, clean life, may be made a perpetual recreation, in the pursuit of simple duty. You can not afford to waste your golden moments—the sweet springtime of your years—in frivolity and nonsense. You should pick your companions, if possible, from those above your intellectual level— from those who can lift you up, not pull you down. At the same time you should be reasonably unselfish in your endeavors to lift up those who are beneath you to your level. When you find that you can be no longer of any use to your companion, nor he to you, cut loose from him—kindly but effectually.

And so, bravely and manfully, bend your young energies to the work of character-building, determined to be a man among men. Your own good sense should teach you the right way—what is necessary for your soul-growth—for your highest welfare. Old age will creep upon you so quickly that you will wonder what has become of the fleeting years. Your golden opportunities, one by one, will slip through your fingers, unless you watch them closely, and you will find yourself with whitened locks and bowed form, standing upon the margin of life's swiftly-flowing river, another failure.

O, thrice happy he, at such a time, who can look back over a life well spent, and can feel as he goes out into the unknown, that he carries with him a bank account of soul that shall last him for all eternity.

THE man who tries to lift himself up by pulling any fellow-being down, is a long way back in the process of evolution.

WHO that has read " David Copperfield,"
that incomparable creation of the master's pen, can ever forget Steerforth,—the
wild, reckless, wicked Steerforth,—and yet
with such streaks of grand manliness running
through his character as to make him at
times almost a god. In his last interview
with Copperfield, he said to him, with the
memory of all their old friendship welling
forth in his heart : " Daisy "—the pet name
he called him by—" Daisy, if anything should
ever separate us, you must think of me at
my best, old boy. Come ! Let us make
that bargain. Think of me at my best."

May not this tender pleading of the wayward Steerforth find a response in other
hearts—in all hearts who read these lines,—
and may it become their rule of action through
all the coming years. How much better
would the world be for it if men and women
thought only of each other at their best.
How it would stimulate all souls to live only

their best, and aspire to be worthy the best thoughts of their fellows. We look upon the cold and silent face of a dead friend or acquaintance, and with hearts aglow with tender pathos, we remember only his good qualities. His virtues shine out brightly and beautifully, eclipsing whatever of fault or weakness, or vice, there may have been in his character. Why should we wait till the winter of death sets its icy seal on heart and lips, before we are ready to think the kindly thought which is as ennobling to ourselves as it would be to the one on whom it is bestowed.

The human race is yet in its moral and spiritual infancy. It is slowly but surely struggling up the hights. On every hand are the foot-sore, and weary, and faltering. Some are borne down with heavy burdens that have been transmitted to them by an ignorant and sinful ancestry. Others seem recklessly squandering the golden hours and opportunities of their lives, and thereby making for themselves beds of thorns for their future years. But if He whom the record informs us " spake not as man spake," could say to the erring one, " Neither do I condemn thee ; go and sin no more," wherefore should the best of us frail mortals presume to sit in judgment upon our fellows ? Can we fathom the mysteries of the erring soul, or weigh the motives that prompt it to action ?

The great want of the world is charity and good will to man. There is something of the best in every life ; and this is the plant we should nurture with the tenderest care. Then let us begin to think of each other "at their best." It is thus that the wilderness of human nature can be made to blossom as the rose.

THE best service most rich men can render to the world is to get out of it and give somebody else a chance. (This does not refer to the rich man who turns his wealth to noble uses.)

EIGHT-HOUR laws are a blessing only to such persons as are capable of making a good use of their unemployed time.

MY ISLAND HOME.

"A mighty realm is the land of dreams,
With steps that haug in the midnight sky;
There are weltering oceans, and trailing streams
That gleam where the dusky valleys lie."

 DWELL in a beautiful land
    On an island than Eden more fair,
Where storm clouds ne'er darken the day,
    Nor pestilence poisons the air.
There are bowers of purple and gold,
    Where the birds sing their sweetest for me,
And magical beauties untold,
    Adorn my dear isle of the sea.

I've a palace of marble and pearl,
    With terraces glittering white,
Mid groves of the orange and lime,
    And fountains that dance in the light;
Near a lake, where the sky overhead
    Is reflected in azure below,
Whose margin is soft to my tread
    Where the myrtle and columbine grow.

The vines bend their emerald heads
    To receive the moist kiss of the wave,
While blushingly watches the rose

From the shore that the bright waters lave.
The zephyrs that sport with the flowers,
   Are laden with many a sweet,
And trippingly glide by the hours,
   Where I dwell in my sylvan retreat.

When weary with heart-aching cares—
   When sorrow and heaviness come,
I step in my light fairy barge,
   And hie to my bright island home.
Loved voices will welcome me there,
   And lift the dark pall from my heart,
Fond Hope take the place of despair,
   And Peace her soft sunlight impart.

Where, do you ask, is this land
   That in beauty an Eden outvies ?
It exists in the realm of my dreams —
   In the ocean of fancy it lies.
Shut out, far away, from the Real,
   From the world and its harassing strife,
I live in the blissful ideal,
   And cull the dream roses of life.

A KIND act performed without the hope of
reward in this world or the next, is a better
evidence of true gentility of soul and a genuine Christian character, than a belief in all
the creeds of Christendom.

LOVE OF THE BEAUTIFUL.

THERE is a ludicrous side to almost every-thing in life—even to the most serious. The useful, the beautiful, the good,—the holiest emotions and aspirations of the soul,—sorrow, affliction, and even death itself,—all come in for their share of ridicule, at times, and are distorted to gratify the fun-loving propensity of human nature.

The esthetic craze is just now the humorous sensation of the hour. The teachings of the great English esthete, Oscar Wilde, the so-called Apostle of the Beautiful, are everywhere distorted to minister to the sense of the ludicrous. Our language is being vitiated into a senseless jargon—with its "too too utterly utter" forms of extravagant expression, and Wilde combinations of meaningless phrases—to add to the already voluminous glossary of American slang.

And yet who shall say there is not a grand thought underlying all this nonsense—a much-needed lesson for the race? It teaches a love for the beautiful—for the adornment and decoration of common things—for the poetry and sentiment, as well as the prosy and practical in life,—just as the soldier, in his peaceful parades and marches, decorates his implements of death with ribbons and flowers.

If he who makes two blades of grass to grow where but one grew before, is entitled to the gratitude of his race ; thrice blessed he who carries a ray of sunshine into any sorrowing heart, or with gladdening words or acts of kindness lightens the burden of any weary life.

There is in this humdrum world of ours—this world of work and worry, of toil and tears—all too little of the ornamental. We delve and dig with our eyes downward, all oblivious of, or indifferent to, the world of beauty around us. Why, Nature herself is a grand old Esthete. She always adorns her roughest and most unsightly places with something of the beautiful—with some flower, or trailing vine, or mossy cushion, to gladden the eye. Even her mountain peaks, robed in eternal snows, wear their crowns of stars ;

and the chafed waves of her ocean wastes flash with the scintillant glories of the night.

There is no home so humble that it may not be made beautiful and attractive by the skillful exercise of taste. The veriest cabin may be turned into a bower of beauty and loveliness, where the soul can revel in the purest joys, and take upon itself something of its beautiful surroundings.

And this, after all, is the highest use and end of life : an esthetic and beautiful soul—a soul adorned with all things lovely—with aspirations outreaching to the skies—with the gentle star-eyed flowers of charity and humanity shedding their fragrance all around, —a soul that is keenly alive to all things good and true—that drinks in the glory of the universe,—that grows wise and beautiful with time, and at last ascends "the golden stair" to a better life beyond.

A SOFT, low word, in kindness spoken—a radiant face beaming with love and sympathy—are dews from heaven, distilling sweet hope and courage to weary-ladened hearts.

SNUGLY ensconsed within a roll of manu-
script, in the northeast upper pigeon
hole of our desk, there lives a little brown
spider, scarcely as large as a common house
fly. Every night it comes out from its
little nest and spins a large beautiful web,—
which, every morning, we ruthlessly brush
away. For two full weeks have we tried to
exhaust the patience of this little insect, but
without avail. With its house in ruins, and
bankrupt in all save perseverance, it patiently goes · to work to repair the loss.
From every indication our little intruder
intends to "fight it out on that line," as long
as life and instinct shall last. Feeling somewhat in a moralizing mood, we propose to
deduce a lesson from the example set by our
little insect toiler. Where is the person
who, in the face of such oft-repeated misfortunes, would have the heart to struggle
on? Would he not sit down and bewail his
hard fate, and suffer the grim specter, Want,

to enter in and become a guest at his fireside? An individual struggling manfully and cheerfully against misfortune is a noble spectacle. The face may be sunbrowned, and the hands sinewy with toil, yet the real diamond of the soul shines all the brighter for its rough setting. He is twice a man who has struggled with, and come off conqueror over, some gréat sorrow. No one can truly appreciate the blessing of health who has never languished on a bed of sickness ; neither can one fully realize how much of heaven it is possible to enjoy on earth who has never felt the pangs of hell in his spirit. The lesson of the spider, then, is one of patient industry. It teaches us to do our best, and then if misfortune comes, to "try again," and to keep on trying, patiently, hopefully, trustingly, as long as life and strength shall last.

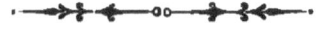

SUFFERING brings strength to strong minds, makes pure souls purer, ennobles noble hearts, and lifts elevated natures to hights sublime.

———

"Self-preservation is the first law of nature," in a moral as well as in a physical sense.

It is better to be born right the first time than to take any chances on the possibility of getting right afterwards.

He who lives meanly will naturally think meanly, and act meanly ; and meanness of any kind is unworthy a noble soul.

It is better for laboring men to have steady employment at low wages than to work one-half the time at high wages.

The human being who hasn't a tear in his heart for another's woe, is undeserving of human sympathy in his own extremity.

Evil doers can be reformed more quickly and effectually by encouragement to do right, than by condemnation for their evil ways.

He serves God best who best serves his fellow men. (Borrowed from the teachings of our elder brothers, Confucius and Jesus.)

POVERTY and riches are but relative terms —gauzy figments of the brain. He only is poor who is poor in soul, and he is poor indeed.

PARENTAL love and tenderness will do more to restrain the wayward feet of an erring child than all the harsh measures ever devised.

THERE would be scarcely any jostling in the journey of life if everybody would but observe the law of the road and "keep to the right."

BEFORE you conclude to do your neighbor an injury, consider well whether it would not add more to your own happiness to befriend him.

THE husband who begrudgingly gives to his wife what is as much hers as his, is deserving of a wife mean enough to steal from his purse while he is asleep.

THE soil is the common heritage of the race, and no man should be allowed to hold any more of it than he can use to the greatest good of himself and the greatest number of his fellows.

IF eternal progression is not an unerring law of nature, then the history of the rocks is a stupendous falsehood,—and if it is such a law, then the nebulous theory of creation is a foregone conclusion.

THE attempt to live in a hundred dollar style on a fifty dollar income—a prevailing weakness of the American people—is a source of more misery than intemperance or war.

THE world's real thinkers, who are comparatively few in numbers, are oftentimes misunderstood, and crucified by those who, as of old, "know not what they do."

THE man who sneers at the honor of woman, or who boasts of his success in any ignoble department of physical life, is a beast. (We beg pardon of the beasts.)

THE unsophisticated young man who wagers his money with a professional gambler at cards, with the idea that he has the least chance to win, exhibits a degree of verdancy that would pass for a fair article of idiocy.

CLEOPATRA'S DREAM,

LO! by Nilus' languid waters
    Fades the dreamy Summer day,
Where, on couch of gold and crimson,
    Egypt's royal daughter lay—
Dreaming lay, while palm and pillar
    Cast their length'ning shadows now,
And the lotus-ladened zephyrs
    Lightly kiss her queenly brow.

Soft, the evening steals upon her,
    As behind the curtained west
Sinks the Day God in his splendor—
    Folds his wooing arms to rest.
Drowsy shapes of dusky Egypt
    Homeward, slow, their burdens bear,
While the boatman's lazy challenge
    Falls upon the quivering air.

Dreams she of her Roman lover—
    He who cast a crown away—
Country, kindred, fame and honor,
    In her captive arms to lay?
Aye! of Antony, her hero,
    Sharer of heart and throne—
He whose ships now homeward sailing,
    Bear her all of love alone.

CLEOPATRA'S DREAM.

Starts she in her sleeping glory,
   And her brown arms, jeweled, bare,
Round and rich in queenly beauty,
   Wildly cleave the slumbrous air.
Beads of perspiration gather
   On her matchless woman's brow,
While her parted lips in anguish
   Tell of heart pangs none may know.

Sure, some vision, dire and dreadful,
   Palls upon her eyes and brain,
Piercing to her being's center,
   With a fiery shaft of pain.
Like a sea, her full orbed bosom
   Swells and falls with pent up ire;
Then her spirit breaks its thraldom,
   And she shrieks in wild despair:

"Charmian, quick, unloose my girdle,
   Give me breath—I faint, I die!
Ho! slaves, bring my royal galley,
   Let us hence from Egypt fly.
O, for vengeance on the traitor,
   And upon his Roman bride;—
Let him never dare—ah, Charmian,
   Stand you closely by my side.

"Do I dream? Is this my palace—
   Yon my smoothly flowing Nile?
Ah, I see—O, great Osiris,
   How I thank thee for thy smile!

O, I've had such fearful vision,—
　　He, my Antony, untrue;
And my heart was nigh to bursting
　　With its fearful weight of woe.

" But 'tis over; yet I tremble—
　　On what brink of fate I stand;
What prophetic bird of evil
　　Hovers o'er this sacred land!
What if true should come my dreaming,
　　And no more my love returns!
Ah! the thought my heart's blood freezes,
　　While my brain with madness burns."

Then she listens, gazing outward,
　　Towards a dim futurity,—
And the Nile, forever onward,
　　Bears its burdens to the sea,—
And she catches from its whispers—
　　Echoing whispers in her soul—
That her reign of love is ended,
　　And her life is near its goal.

www.ingramcontent.com/pod-product-compliance
Lightning Source LLC
Chambersburg PA
CBHW030810020726
47499CB00006B/1852